The
Strange things
RED
are happening next door
SHOE

Ursula Dubosarsky

WALKER BOOKS

Published by arrangement with Allen and Unwin

First published in Great Britain 2015 by Walker Books Ltd
87 Vauxhall Walk, London SE11 5HJ

2 4 6 8 10 9 7 5 3 1

Text © 2006 by Ursula Dubosarky
Cover illustration © 2015 by Rebecca Stadtlander

The right of Ursula Dubosarky to be identified as author of this
work has been asserted by her in accordance with the
Copyright, Designs and Patents Act 1988

This book has been typeset in Bembo

Printed and bound in Great Britain by Clays Ltd, St Ives plc

British Library Cataloguing in Publication Data:
a catalogue record for this book is available from the British Library

ISBN 978-1-4063-5874-2

www.walker.co.uk

For Susie Bridge, dear old friend xxx

and with special thanks to Professor John Stephens and Macquarie University, in appreciation of all the highly valued support during the writing of this book

ONCE UPON A TIME...

*M*atilda stood at the bedroom doorway in the early morning, watching her older sister Frances, who was just waking up. Her face looked like someone else's when she was asleep. It was only when she opened her eyes that Matilda knew it was really her.

Frances rolled over on her shoulder and then she blinked. That was enough. Matilda bounded into the room like a runaway sheep and jumped in the bed with her sister, pulling the bedclothes over her head.

"What are you doing?" Frances yawned.

Under the eiderdown Matilda squirmed closer. Her voice was muffled in feathers.

"Will you read me a story?"

Frances was good at reading stories, much better than their mother or father or their big sister, Elizabeth.

"Oh, Matilda," sighed Frances.

"Please, Frances?" said Matilda. "Please?"

Matilda couldn't read by herself yet, or at least, only little words. Looking at all those black strokes and circles at school gave her a headache.

"Oh all right." Frances gave up. "Get me a book then."

Matilda leaned down to the bookshelf that was between their beds, and tugged out a book of fairytales that she had been given at Christmas.

"Which one?" Frances took the book and began flipping over the pages.

"I don't care," said Matilda under the eiderdown. "Any one."

"I know." Frances half sat up. "Let's get the book to choose."

She lifted the book of fairytales up in the air and waved it about. The pages swished back and forth above them, making a little wind. At last she let the book fall open in one place, brought it back down and read out the title.

"'The Red Shoes,'" she announced. "All right?"

"All right," agreed Matilda.

Frances started to read. She had a low humming

sort of voice, like a quiet lawnmower. The story was about a little girl called Karen. There were three Karens in Matilda's class at school, and now she saw them all at once but somehow mixed up together, one with long blonde plaits, one with huge dark brown eyes and one with millions and millions of freckles.

The little Karen in the story was so poor she had to wear wooden shoes that were hard and tight and made her feet red with blisters.

"Poor little Karen." Matilda wiggled her own pink soft toes.

Then poor little Karen's mother died, and the shoemaker's wife made Karen some shoes out of dirty red leather to wear to the funeral. A rich old lady going by saw her at the funeral and said, "If you will give me the little girl, I will take care of her."

"Lucky little Karen," said Matilda happily.

"Shhh."

Little Karen thought the rich lady liked her because of her red shoes, but really the old lady thought they were hideous and burnt them when Karen wasn't looking.

That's mean, thought Matilda, but she didn't say it out loud, because Frances was looking cross.

The rich old lady dressed little Karen in clean clothes and taught her to read and sew, and everyone said she

was pretty. But when little Karen looked in the mirror, the mirror said, "You are more than pretty – you are beautiful."

"But mirrors can't talk," said Matilda quickly. "Can they?"

"They can in stories," said Frances.

Matilda shook her head. Mirrors couldn't talk. They're just glass, she told herself firmly. They're not real.

One day a princess was travelling through the land where little Karen lived, and little Karen saw her. The princess had the most beautiful red shoes, the best the best the best in the world.

"Does little Karen get them?" asked Matilda excitedly.

"Just listen, will you?" said Frances.

It was time for Karen's confirmation—

"What's that?" asked Matilda.

"Something you do in church." Frances gritted her teeth.

"But what is it?" persisted Matilda.

"You wear a white dress and you go to church and they say prayers and things," explained Frances.

It was time for Karen's confirmation—

Matilda thought about the white dress. It sounded like a wedding. There was a photo of their parents' wedding on top of the piano, their mother in a long *white dress and her father in a black suit. And there was their mother's friend, Yvonne, standing just behind them in a floppy hat, surrounded by flowers. But how could a little girl like Karen be getting married? Matilda looked at Frances. She decided not to ask.*

It was time for Karen's confirmation, and the old lady took her to the shoemaker to get some shoes. The shoemaker showed her a pair of beautiful shiny red shoes. Karen wanted them very much and luckily for her the old lady was so old she couldn't see colours any more and she bought them. Of course, if she had known they were red she wouldn't have, because you're not allowed to wear red shoes to church.

"Why can't you wear red shoes to church?" Matilda was puzzled. She didn't mean to interrupt, but she couldn't help it.

"That's the rule," replied Frances in a monotone.

"This is a long story," said Matilda.

So little Karen wore the shiny red shoes to her confirmation and everyone thought she was very wicked to wear red shoes to church. When the rich old lady found out, she said to Karen that she wasn't allowed to wear them any more to church, only black ones.

Only black. Matilda had black shoes for school, but she still couldn't tie her laces.

"On the following Sunday," Frances continued, "there was Communion. Karen looked first at the black shoes, then at the red ones – looked at the red ones again, and put them on."

"What's Communion?" asked Matilda in a very tiny voice. "Sorry," she added.

"It's just something else in church," said Frances, shrugging. "I don't know. I think it's something Catholics do."

Matilda nodded. There was a Catholic school not far from their own. Matilda sometimes peeked through the fence on the way home to look at the beautiful white statues of Jesus and Mary in the asphalt playground, like shining swans on a hard grey lake. There was a church next to the school, and on Saturdays and Sundays it was always full of people because Catholics loved going to church all the time, but the priest spoke a different language that only God could understand. A girl at school called Isabel told her all about it. Isabel knew because her auntie was a Catholic. Catholics really believe, Isabel said. Doesn't everyone believe? wondered Matilda, because she believed, at least she thought she did. Not like Catholics, said Isabel.

The room was dark and shadowy and the blinds waved in the morning breeze. Outside there was a tree with tiny red berries that brushed against the glass. They looked like lollies, but their father said they were poisonous, they could kill you if you ate them. They were worse than redback spiders. In the wind at night those branches made scraping sounds, and sometimes Matilda thought it was someone in the garden digging her grave.

"At the church door," Frances went on, "stood an old crippled soldier leaning on a crutch; he had a wonderfully long beard, more red than white, and he bowed down to the ground."

Matilda pulled herself up to look at the book. She wanted to see if there was a picture of the soldier. She had never seen a soldier with a long red-and-white beard. All the soldiers she had seen had no beards and hardly any hair, although some of them had only one leg or one arm. But there was no picture, just black letters on the page, like hundreds of tiny footprints.

Karen put out her little foot too. "Dear me, what pretty dancing shoes!" said the soldier. "Sit fast, when you dance," said he, addressing the shoes, and slapping the soles with his hands.

"Why is he talking to the shoes?" Matilda frowned.

They were magic shoes, said Frances. When little Karen wore them, she couldn't stop dancing. Even when she wanted to stop, she couldn't, the shoes wouldn't let her.

Matilda put her face into the pillow. It smelt of skin and hair. She stopped listening to the words for a while, and just listened to the sound of Frances's voice instead. Frances read: "One morning Karen danced past a door that she knew well; they were singing a psalm inside and a coffin was being carried out covered with flowers. Then she knew that she was forsaken by everyone and damned by the angel of God."

"Don't cut off my head," said Karen, "for then I could not repent of my sin. But cut off my feet with the red shoes."

"But she didn't do anything wrong!" said Matilda. She sat upright, stiff with shock. "She didn't do anything!"

The executioner chopped off Karen's feet with an axe and gave her some wooden feet instead and a pair of crutches.

"He chopped off her feet?"

Matilda felt sick. What would it be like to have wooden feet? She remembered that day in town with their mother, when they had seen a little girl in a tartan coat with metal where her socks should be. It's polio, said their mother, don't look, girls, don't look. But Matilda had looked, even as her mother pulled her away, at the little girl with metal legs and crutches and heard the terrible thumping as she walked. Don't look, don't look, said their mother, that child will never run again.

"This story is too sad," Matilda scowled. "I don't like it."

"Hang on." Frances turned the page. "There's a picture now."

Matilda peered over Frances's shoulder. Opposite the print there was a coloured drawing on shiny paper, of a moon with a face and a long, long beard. It was pale and strange, as though someone had painted it in with a paintbrush.

"That's the old soldier," said Frances. "The one who said the shoes were pretty."

"But it looks like the moon." Matilda touched it with her fingers. "He looks like the moon."

Frances didn't answer.

"I don't like this story," said Matilda definitely. "I don't want to learn to read if stories are like that."

"It's got a happy ending." Frances glanced down at the last few lines.

"Like what?"

Frances read: "Her soul flew on the sunbeams to Heaven and no one was there who asked after the Red Shoes."

There was a short silence.

"That's it?" said Matilda, in disbelief.

"That's the end," admitted Frances.

"That means she's dead!" said Matilda, outraged. "If she goes to heaven, she's dead. What's so happy about that?"

"Well, that's the end."

Frances closed the book. She climbed out of bed, found her slippers and headed down the hall to the kitchen for breakfast.

She's not happy if she's dead, thought Matilda, flopping on her back and staring up at the ceiling where a big crack was growing like a giant spiderweb. That's a silly thing to say. I don't like that story at all. Why shouldn't little Karen have her beautiful red shoes?

Their mother had some red shoes, with golden buckles and shiny black heels. They made a clicking sound on the pavement, like a tap-dancer. Matilda loved those shoes.

"Red shoes," whispered Matilda under the blanket.

And she lay there quite still, listening to the sounds of the morning, but somewhere inside her she thought she might be afraid.

The Sydney Morning Herald

> *Thursday*, APRIL 8, 1954 <

Annihilation Of All Life: Prophecy Now Possible

———•———

NEW YORK, April 7 (A.A.P.) — The successful testing of the hydrogen bomb has made possible Professor Albert Einstein's prophecy of a weapon capable of annihilating life on earth, says William Laurence, the science expert of the "New York Times".

> *Friday*, APRIL 9, 1954 <

ONLY DEFENCE TO H-BOMB IS TO LIVE UNDERGROUND

———•———

"There is no defence against atomic weapons unless humanity is prepared to live, work and grow food deep beneath the surface of the earth," Professor Mark Oliphant said in his address at the Town Hall last night.

The Sydney Morning Herald

TWO MORE POLIO CASES

Two cases of poliomyelitis were reported in New South Wales yesterday a Health department spokesman said last night.

The spokesman said that the cases, a child and a 20 year old man, were reported from Rockdale and Shellharbour.

There have been 326 cases of polio, including seven deaths, reported in NSW since the beginning of the year.

MRS. GRILLS DENIED LEAVE TO APPEAL

The Court of Criminal Appeal in a reserved judgment yesterday refused Mrs. Caroline Grills leave to appeal against her conviction for the attempted murder of her sister in law Mrs. Eveline Lundberg by thallium poisoning.

Mrs. Grills, 63, of Garish Street Gladesville is the wife of a city estate agent.

She was convicted at the Central Criminal Court last year on a charge of having administered thallium to Mrs. Lundberg, 67, at Redfern on April 20 1953 with intent to murder her.

She was sentenced to death.

One

IN A HOUSE FAR AWAY, right at the end of a long dusty road deep in the bush at the back of Palm Beach, lived three sisters with their mother, their father, and sometimes their Uncle Paul. The three sisters were called Elizabeth, Frances and Matilda.

Elizabeth was fifteen. She had long hair in plaits and she didn't go to school. She used to go to school but one day she'd come home with her plaits tied up on top of her head with a white ribbon and said she wasn't going back. Their mother had called the doctor and the doctor agreed with Elizabeth.

"She needs a rest," the doctor said, stroking Elizabeth's tight hand. "She's having a nervous breakdown."

Their mother sat down on a chair in the kitchen and cried.

After a while Elizabeth said, "I am the one having the nervous breakdown, not you."

So their mother got up from the chair, but she was not pleased with Elizabeth. She thought Elizabeth was making it up.

"You can't have a nervous breakdown when you are only fifteen," said their mother.

That's what she told their father on the telephone. He was in the merchant navy, far away on a ship in the middle of the ocean, looking for the enemy with his binoculars.

"YOU CAN'T HAVE A NERVOUS BREAKDOWN WHEN YOU ARE ONLY FIFTEEN!" their mother shouted down the telephone.

Frances, the middle daughter, was eleven. She had grey eyes and even her hair looked grey, a sort of koala colour. She didn't talk much, not when adults were there, anyway, but that made everybody listen to her more. When she finally did say something, it was almost exciting.

"She speaks!" Uncle Paul would cry.

Then everyone would stare at her, and of course she would forget what she was going to say, and she'd wish she'd never opened her mouth in the first place.

Matilda was the youngest. Matilda was six. Some six-year-olds are not sneaky, but Matilda was. Her hair was black and so were her eyes. Even her blood was nearly black and seeped out very, very slowly when she cut herself. She was like a spy.

"You're not brave enough to be a spy," her friend Floreal told her. "You're cowards, all of you."

"My father is brave," Matilda retorted. "He was in the war."

"The war is over now," said Floreal. "And he's not so brave, anyway. I have seen him go white in the face when a big lizard crawled up the back step."

This was true, and it was hard to see how a man who was frightened of a lizard would be much good in a battle. Floreal was blunt and truthful, and remembered all sorts of things that other people forgot. He was an unusual friend, because he was invisible. He was also very small, only about as tall as a book. If he had been flat, he could have been a bookmark.

"I still think my father is brave," Matilda said to herself. "Anyone can be frightened of a lizard."

The lizard had crawled up the back step one Sunday afternoon when Uncle Paul was visiting and they were eating roast lamb and potatoes and peas and onions for Sunday lunch. Uncle Paul was their father's little brother. He used to come and stay with them when he didn't have to work. Uncle Paul played the piano in restaurants lit by candles while people danced round and round on a shiny floor. He lived in a hotel in the city with clean sheets every day.

They looked alike, the two brothers, but Uncle Paul

was more handsome because his hair was longer and he led a wild life. He was hairy altogether, with curling eyelashes like a doll and thick eyebrows, and he even had a moustache with little streaks of silver in it. He had one lock of grey hair on the right side of his head. It had been there since he was a child. It shows I'm a genius, he told them. No matter what I do, it keeps growing back.

Usually Uncle Paul came to visit when their father was away, because it was hard to have two large men in one house. They ate too much, and also when they were both there at once the laundry overflowed with pairs of shoes and no one could ever find anything. They used to fight as well, not punching each other, but bellowing even when they were standing face to face. They argued about cigarettes and aeroplanes and how to cut the lawn. Brothers will always fight, sighed their mother, it's in the Bible.

It was because of Elizabeth that their father was at home that Sunday when the lizard crawled up the back step. He should have been on the deck of his ship but he had come especially because he was worried about Elizabeth. He wanted her to go back to school and do her exams. Elizabeth had a big brain, everyone said so. There was no one else in the family with a brain like hers.

"You are all of you so stupid," said Floreal, "except for Elizabeth."

That Sunday it was two months already since Elizabeth's nervous breakdown. Two months is a long time to stay at home when you are only fifteen. Elizabeth didn't go out to see any of her friends from school. She just sat around the house, reading the newspaper and watching her mother. Some days she took a plastic bucket and went down through the thick twisted bush to the beach and filled it with pale sand. Then she brought it back and dumped the sand in the front yard on the flower bed. Now there was a big pile of sand and the flowers underneath were dying.

Lamb and potatoes and peas and onions – how rich it smelt, how warm! Like spring and summer and winter and autumn all mixed up at once. Matilda sprinkled salt onto her potatoes so they looked like the Snowy Mountains. She forked each mountain whole into her mouth and swallowed them one by one, until she finished the entire range. She felt very good and strong.

"You're greedy," said Floreal. "You're going to be sick."

Matilda poked out her tongue to where she thought he was. She didn't like it when Floreal talked to her when other people were there. It made things difficult. But Floreal did as he pleased.

"I saw some men go in the big house next door this morning," said Matilda.

"Really?" Their mother looked up, alert. The house next door had two storeys and a long wide front garden and a side driveway for cars. It's like a film star's house, their mother said, but nobody lived there, not even a film star, because it was a holiday home. Lots of the houses in the streets around them were like that. In the summer people

came in cars and had parties in the houses and trailed down
to the beach. But the rest of the year the streets were empty
as a ghost town. There were more trees than houses, more
possums than people, their mother said. It's like living at
the ends of the earth, said their mother, and in fact it was.

"What did you see?" their father asked Matilda, as they
finished off the lamb and the last drops of gravy.

"Some men came in a car," Matilda answered. "They
looked funny."

She had been playing by herself in the front yard when
they came. She had watched them through the fence but
they hadn't seen her.

"What sort of funny?" asked their mother.

"What sort of car?" asked their father.

"I don't know," said Matilda. "It was black. They had
black hats and coats and umbrellas and they went inside."

"Why umbrellas?" Uncle Paul raised his eyebrows. "It
hasn't rained for weeks."

That was true. It was dry as dry, and the red earth was
like powder and rock. You weren't allowed to water the
garden. The newspaper said you just had to get used to
grass being yellow instead of green. Matilda liked that idea.
Perhaps you could get used to things being different colours
altogether – the huge ocean could be pink and the sand
could be purple.

"Weren't there any women?" asked their mother,
sounding desperate, because she was lonely at the ends of
the earth.

"There wasn't a mother," Matilda said with certainty. "Or any children."

"Or an auntie or a granny or a dog," smiled Uncle Paul. "Or a little blue budgie in his cage."

Their father stood up from the table and went over to the door that led from the dining room to the back yard. He pushed open the flyscreen and looked out, standing on the back step. They could hear the cicadas crying from the tall trees surrounding them, like hundreds of heartbeats. The big house next door seemed to wave in the afternoon sunlight.

"Nobody there now," he said. "And the blinds are down."

Through the open door, wind came in from the Pacific Ocean. They couldn't see the waves from where they lived, but they heard it and smelt it, all the time. Uncle Paul smiled again from under his silvery moustache. He was looking at their mother. She was wearing tiny crimson earrings, like drops of blood.

Then their father made a funny sound. "Look!" he said, and his voice was hoarse.

They all got up from the table, except Elizabeth, and looked.

A large, grey-green goanna was slowly climbing up the concrete step, out from the tangled bush, through the afternoon heat towards their house, towards their father's feet. Its mouth was hanging open, and it raised one of its knobbled legs in the air, spreading its toes apart.

"Calm down," said Uncle Paul to their father, because

their father was shaking as though he had a fever. He wasn't afraid of Germans or bombs but he was afraid of lizards. He was afraid of all animals.

"He's a coward," said Floreal.

"Do something, Paul," said their mother urgently. "It's horrible. Do something! Shoo it away."

Now they were all crowding around the door, looking down at the goanna, except Elizabeth. She put her elbows on the table and yawned.

"Can we catch it?" begged Matilda, excited. "I could take it to school for the Pet Parade."

There was to be a Pet Parade at school that week. The prize for the most unusual pet was a huge round green and yellow and white and pink lollipop that sat on her teacher's desk. It had every colour in the rainbow, the teacher told them, and it was called an all-day sucker, which meant it would last all day long if you were careful not to chew it. God must have made it, thought Matilda, it must be what they eat in heaven. If Matilda could catch the goanna and take it to school in a bucket, she might win! She bent down and reached out her hand. If she could just get hold of its tail...

Uncle Paul stepped forward and made a kicking motion with his foot.

"Cha-cha-cha!" he grunted through his teeth and kicked again.

The goanna did not move. Its front leg was suspended in the air. It was still as stone, its mouth gaping and its eyes fixed.

"Don't!" said Matilda, tugging Uncle Paul. "Don't scare him! Let me catch him!"

"It'll bite you, Mattie!" warned their mother.

The goanna raised its head calmly as a judge, its tongue flicking in and out of its mouth. It hesitated, looking at Matilda through small black eyes as though considering what to do.

"Gara-gara-gara!" said Uncle Paul, showing his teeth.

"Don't!" Matilda wailed.

The goanna made a decision. It wheeled its heavy body around and leapt down the step, running on all four legs surprisingly swiftly, back into the high weeds at the edge of the yard, the dark growth beyond the fence.

"What did you do that for?" Matilda shouted at Uncle Paul.

"Poor Mattie," said Uncle Paul. "Nature lover."

"It must have smelt the meat," said their mother.

Their father walked out of the room. They heard him in the kitchen, opening the fridge, taking out a bottle of beer. He was ashamed because he was so afraid. Elizabeth laid her head on the table. Frances sat down and ate a spoonful of peas.

Uncle Paul leaned over to Matilda and gave her shoulders a squeeze, but she was too angry. She turned her back to him, her face squashed up in crossness.

"Don't think the goanna would have liked school much," he said.

"Go away!" mumbled Matilda.

Why did he do that? She could have won the lollipop, she knew she could have. But none of them cared, not a bit. Now she wouldn't tell them anything more about the people she'd seen in the house next door, about the big black car and the men in their suits and black hats.

There were lots of things she wasn't going to tell them now. There were so many other things they didn't know that she knew. She certainly wasn't going to tell them about the gun.

Two

ONE OF THE MEN Matilda had seen going into the big house next door had a gun. It was black and curved, hanging from his belt. Matilda knew it was a gun, a real gun. It was not the first time that she had seen one.

She had seen a gun just like it in the house of the mad old man who lived on the other side of them. Nobody knew she had been in the house of the mad old man. Nobody saw her and she didn't tell anybody. This was partly because she was sneaky, but more because her mother would have been cross. The old man was strange as well as mad, and her mother had told her not to speak to strangers. But sometimes Matilda couldn't help herself.

She hadn't meant to, it had just happened. She had been out in the front garden one afternoon all alone playing with some pebbles, singing a little song she'd made up about a bus and a train, when the mad old man came up the path to get his letters. He didn't shake his walking stick at her as he did at her mother. Instead he stared through his scrunched-up eyes and said, "What are you doing? Eh?"

"Playing," said Matilda.

"Would you like a chocolate biscuit?" asked the old man. "Eh?"

"Yes," said Matilda.

"Come on, then," said the mad old man, gesturing.

He was very old. His arms and legs were covered with long white hairs and his face was all brown and crushed. When he walked he hardly lifted up his feet, and his shoes sounded like rustling newspaper as they scraped along the ground, and then his stick as well. He was wearing a red woollen hat like a lady, and he had a pencil stuck behind his ear.

Matilda put the pebbles into her pocket and followed him down the concrete path to his front door. There were ants scurrying all over the ground and they bit her toes, hundreds of little black stinging ants.

"What's your name?" he asked her as he pushed open the rusting screen door. "Eh?"

"Matilda," she said, trying to wipe the ants from her feet.

The door banged shut behind them. Inside the house it was dark and it smelt of cats and something else. It feels wet, thought Matilda, like a cave. There was a reddish cat lying almost flat on the table in the kitchen, and another one, a brown and grey one, curled on top of the stove. They didn't open their eyes but she knew they were alive because she could see their stomachs moving up and down.

"Here you are," said the old man.

Apart from the cats, the kitchen was neat, neater than theirs. There was a folded tea towel next to the sink and a shining blue metal teapot. There was an open newspaper on the kitchen table, and next to it a biscuit tin. The old man picked it up and pulled off the lid. He had to do it with one hand, because with the other hand he was leaning on his wooden stick, which was twisted at the top like Little Bo Peep's. His hand shook so much as he opened the tin, Matilda thought it was never going to happen. But then:

"Go on, take one," said the old man at last, holding the tin out. "Get on with it, will you?"

The biscuits sat in layers underneath a piece of grease-proof paper. Matilda was disappointed that they weren't chocolate-covered, but only chocolate-coloured. She reached out her hand and took one.

"Have another," he said, rattling the tin. "Eh!"

So she did.

"Have another," he said again, sounding angry.

Matilda thought she might be going to cry. She took another one and put all three of them in her mouth at once.

"Come in here," said the old man, beckoning as he shuffled into the living room with his stick. "Here's something I bet you've never seen. Eh?"

Matilda followed him into the room. There was a green velvet sofa and two armchairs and on every cushion another cat. There was a long mirror in one corner, mouldy with gold edges. Matilda could just see herself in it, in the shadows.

The old man stood next to the fireplace. He had dropped his stick and was leaning forward. In the dark, his red hat was like a flame. There were bookshelves all along the walls, filled with rows and rows of empty beer bottles.

"What do you think of this, eh?"

The old man lunged over to the mantelpiece and seized a huge silver sword curved like a new moon, which was hanging on a hook above the fireplace where there should have been a picture of trees and a river and cows eating grass.

Matilda screamed and jumped back. The mad old man stood in the middle of the room and whizzed the sword through the air. It sounded like a bird flying by very fast.

"Bet you never seen one of these," said the old man, suddenly lowering the sword to the floor. "Eh?"

"No," admitted Matilda.

"Come here and have a proper look," he said. Then, because she seemed to be hesitating, "Come on, come on, don't muck about!"

Matilda went over. She looked at the sword. It was like a giant knife for cutting up roast chicken. She wondered if the old man might be about to kill her with it, chop her head off. She waited for him to say something. There were bits of chocolate biscuit stuck to her teeth and she tried to get them off with her tongue. She wished she could go home.

"Got it from a Jap," said the old man. "It's mine now, ha!"

"Were you in the war?" asked Matilda.

"Ha!" replied the old man.

"My dad was in the war," said Matilda.

"Ha!" said the old man.

Matilda wasn't sure if she believed in the war. Maybe the war never really happened, like a film at the cinema which looked real and felt real but wasn't. Films were just dreams, flashes of light in the dark, like stars.

"Ha!" said the old man again, and he held the sword right up to his face, the blade on his cheek.

Matilda had been born when the war was over. That meant she was different to her sisters. Now there would be no more wars, their mother told them, since Matilda was born. But Matilda was not so sure.

"Got to watch those Japs," said the old man. "Got to watch 'em. The Japs. And the Reds, don't forget them. You got to watch the Reds."

Well, he didn't have to tell Matilda that. Matilda knew all about the Reds. Down at the bend in their street there was a block of bush, so thick with tall gum trees and a great grey rock broken in pieces scattered about at the front. There were cowboys and Red Indians hiding in there, with guns and bows and arrows and they would shoot her if they could.

"Which is meaner?" asked Matilda curiously. "The Reds or the Japs?"

"I know what I'm talking about," muttered the old man, seeming not to hear. "Got to be careful."

Matilda waited. She wanted to go home but she didn't know how. She didn't want to look at the sword or the mad old man and the place where his eyes had disappeared into folds of skin, so she looked around the room instead.

She looked at the fireplace and she looked at the cats, and she looked at the floor and the hole in the carpet in the shape of a lake. Then she looked over to the other side of the room and she saw it. In one corner, there was a little round table with a tray on top of it, and on top of the tray was the gun. It lay there, gleaming like fresh licorice.

"Want another biscuit?" snapped the old man. "Eh?"

"No thank you," said Matilda.

"Well, off you go then," said the mad old man, irritated again.

He had his back to her, he was sliding the sword into its scabbard, on the wall above the mantelpiece.

Matilda ran away from the mad old man's house, out the door and down the path covered with ants and back inside her own front yard.

She didn't tell anybody about where she'd been, or the sword or the gun or especially the chocolate biscuits. She just ran away as fast as she could, back to her own safe house.

Three

AFTER THEY FINISHED LUNCH, the day the lizard crawled up the back step, their father returned to his ship and Uncle Paul went back to his hotel in the city to play the piano, and the girls and their mother had the house to themselves again. When the men had gone, their mother was sad.

"Why does it have to be like this?" she said, sitting down in the chair in the kitchen, the same chair she always sat in when things went wrong.

That night Matilda couldn't sleep. She sat up in bed and put her face against the glass of the window. In the big house next door the lights were all on under the blinds. How did they breathe, if they never opened the windows? She looked over at Frances. She was asleep, flat on her back, as though she was staring at the ceiling with her eyes closed. It made Matilda feel nervous.

"Floreal?" she whispered into the dark room.

There was no answer, but that didn't mean he wasn't there.

He could be standing right there staring at me, thought Matilda, and I wouldn't know.

What colour would Floreal's eyes be? Maybe they had no colour, but were like balls of ice.

"Floreal?"

When Matilda had first got to know Floreal, she had thought he might be her guardian angel. But there was nothing patient or kind or at all angelic about Floreal. Matilda had the feeling that if she found herself about to be eaten by a shark or hit on the head by a falling coconut, Floreal wouldn't do anything at all.

Sometimes it seemed to Matilda that she had known Floreal all her life, although she knew that was not the case. Floreal had first spoken to her just three months ago.

It was the day after Boxing Day. She and Elizabeth and Frances had been lying in the living room, listening to the radio. It was a strange afternoon, they all felt strange. They had been on a picnic to the Basin the day before and their blood was warm with sunburn. Elizabeth was on the couch, Frances was sprawled out on the floor drawing and Matilda sat sleepily in an armchair with her book of fairy tales in her lap, looking at the pictures.

The radio was in a brown box which sat in front of the fireplace. When you turned it on, it crackled, like bacon spitting in a pan. Their mother and father were having an afternoon rest in their bedroom, so the volume of the radio could not be very loud, just a slippery murmur from the square soft space where the sound was made.

They spent a lot of time listening to the radio. Normally they listened to a children's program called "The Argonauts", named after Jason and the Argonauts, who sailed around the world in the olden days, looking for the Golden Fleece. The Argonauts on the radio were in a club, and they all had different voices and funny names, like Pallas 21 or Arachne 93.

Sometimes Matilda imagined the Argonauts were actual little people who lived inside the radio. She thought of them sitting around a tiny kitchen table, just like their own, reading things out from tiny newspapers, arguing or acting out plays. But when she knelt down and peered inside the back of the radio, there was only darkness and a bitter electrical smell. Perhaps they were just voices, like Floreal. Could a person be only a voice? You don't have to see things to believe them. Like God, thought Matilda.

That afternoon, when Floreal first spoke to her, someone inside the radio was reading out a story all about a brave doctor who saved lives in the jungle. It went on and on and on. Matilda wished they would sing a song. The

Argonauts had a special rowing song, when you could pretend you were on a boat.

"Row! Row! Row!" hummed Matilda.

Elizabeth gave her a kick.

"I can't hear," she said.

Matilda stopped humming. Her skin was peeling from sunburn, she pulled off a long translucent piece from the top of her arm. On and on droned the story about the brave doctor. She began to feel distant and slightly airborne. In fact, she fell asleep. She only realized that the radio had been turned off and the others had gone, when the corner of the book in her lap began sticking into her ear and she woke up. She shifted in irritation and threw the book into the middle of the floor.

Then she heard a voice.

"You nearly hit me!"

Not for a moment did Matilda think it was her imagination or that she was hearing things. She sat up straight and said, "I didn't know you were there."

It was Floreal. He was one of the Argonauts and he'd come right out of the radio. His whole name was Floreal 22. He didn't actually ever say so, but Matilda knew. There were some things Matilda knew, just as she knew he was very small and flat, although he never mentioned it himself.

But he mentioned lots of other things. Lots and lots and lots. At first she was glad, she liked to hear him talk. He talked about everything, there was nothing he didn't know about. He talked until the sun came down and the windowpane turned grey, then blue, then black with lost light. At last Matilda was worn out with listening. She wished he would go back inside the radio, then she could just turn him off.

Finally she said, "I think I better go now."

"Suit yourself," said Floreal and his voice disappeared at once.

Matilda stood up, shaking her legs from pins and needles. She went over to the radio and put her hand on the top of it. It was still warm with dying electricity.

"Hallo?" she said, in the dark and quiet house. "Floreal? Are you there?"

Matilda thought that she had offended him and he would not come back. But he did.

Four

THE NIGHT AFTER THE lizard crawled up the back step, Elizabeth paced up and down in her bedroom with a terrible restlessness. I can't stand it, she thought. I have to go out.

Elizabeth was a night walker. She went out walking at night because she couldn't sleep. She undressed, put on her nightie and lay down on the bed, but she did not fall asleep and she did not wake up. It was as though she had forgotten how. It was the opposite of Rip Van Winkle, or Sleeping Beauty. Could such a thing be possible? Could you be awake for twenty years, instead of asleep? It was not the sort of thing she could ask the doctor.

"You need to rest," that's what the doctor said.

He came to the house to see her. He had a black bag, just like doctors in storybooks. He gave her medicine to take.

"You've been trying too hard," said the doctor. "You must stop trying."

He meant at her schoolwork, she supposed. What else could he mean? She couldn't really remember much about school, so perhaps he was right. There was a pile of books on the shelf in her room. Her English teacher, Mr Wells, had brought them round to the house when he'd heard about the nervous breakdown. He'd come to the door, and her mother had asked him in and made him a cup of tea.

Elizabeth knew he was there, because she heard his voice, but she wouldn't come out of her room. She climbed inside the wardrobe, sat on top of all the shoes, and shut the door, waiting in the smell of leather and sweat for Mr Wells to go. She felt so cold in there. She shivered and her teeth chattered, until she had to hold her jaw closed with her hands.

"Why don't you go and see your friends?" her mother said. "Have a chat. Go out together."

But Elizabeth couldn't remember having any friends. She didn't know what her mother was talking about. The only thing she remembered clearly was the bus – the rumble, the lurching movement, the silver-edged steps up and down. That day she had come home with the white ribbon tied on top of her head, she had got off the bus with one sentence inside her: I won't go back. And she hadn't – not so far.

"I won't go back," she told her mother. "I don't want to go."

"Aren't you bored?" her mother said. "Sitting around here all day?"

Elizabeth was not bored. For one thing, there was the newspaper. Now she was at home, she could read it all day long. She had always liked reading the newspaper, but since her nervous breakdown she had begun to read every single word, really every word. All the conflicts, crimes, unknown names, excitements and miseries, all those numbers and letters and reports of rain and snow. She read the legal reports and the obituaries and the medical notices and the houses for sale and the employment columns and the entertainments. Everything seemed to fit into a mysterious and beautiful pattern, connected like fine strands of coloured cotton strung across each other to form curving parabolas.

"It all means something," she nodded, "but nobody knows what."

She wasn't bored. When she wasn't reading the newspaper, she watched her mother. She could see her mother thinking all the time. Sometimes she wanted to reach forward and touch her hand and say, Stop thinking, it's no good, just stop it. In the afternoon, at about one o'clock, after a morning's housework, her mother would lie down for a while in bed with the curtains drawn. But she wasn't sleeping, Elizabeth could tell. She was lying on her side, thinking. What did she think about? I live at the ends of the Earth, her mother said, without a friend in the world, except for Yvonne and she's a thousand miles away.

Yvonne was their mother's great friend. They'd been at school together and then at work together, in a big office in town during the war, when all the men were fighting far away. There was a photo of her mother and Yvonne on the way to work, all dressed up, taken by a street photographer. Such smart clothes they used to wear! Such hats, such shoes.

"What did you do in the office?" Elizabeth asked, staring at the bright eyes, the shy, strong smiles.

"Oh, office things," said her mother dismissively.

When Yvonne was nineteen, she got married to a man from New Zealand and off she went to live there, near his family. Then their mother got married too and went to live at the ends of the earth. My very best friend, their mother said, and I haven't seen her in fifteen years.

Their mother wrote long letters to Yvonne on thin sheets of paper, like flakes of sweet pastry. Yvonne wrote back, usually postcards. "Yvonne doesn't waste words," said their mother. "She gets on with the job." "What job?" asked Elizabeth. Yvonne worked in a paint shop now. Yvonne's husband was killed in the war, in the Solomon Islands. "That's his story," said their mother. She didn't believe it. "He just took off with a native girl," said their mother, "and pretended he was dead." Like a zombie? thought Elizabeth. She had read about zombies in the Sunday papers. The living dead. "He was a shocker, alive or dead," said their mother. "Yvonne deserved better than him. Yvonne deserved the best."

"But what happens to her children when she's in the paint shop?" asked Matilda. Their mother looked after them, who would look after Yvonne's children? But Yvonne didn't have any children. "Not that you know about," said their father. "Oh excuse me," said their mother. "I've only got one friend, and she's a thousand miles away, so just leave her alone." Chopping, washing, dusting, sweeping and the sound of the radio.

"Elizabeth has to go to school," said her father.

"But I don't want to go," said Elizabeth.

Elizabeth would not go back to school, ever, no matter what her father said. Why did he want her to go to school so much? They couldn't make her, Elizabeth knew. It was the law. She was fifteen. She could get a job. There were plenty advertised under "Women and Girls", columns and columns of them. Elizabeth had circled a few with a red pencil. "A CAPABLE YOUNG LADY who is interested in FIGURE WORK" was one. "Girls or young women, positions requiring average ability and common sense. Good prospects for suitable types" was another. Or "Catholic Girls, 15 years. Required all Departments" or even "Girls about 18 yrs age wanted for bottling and labelling". She was fifteen, but she could look older. But the doctor said she was not ready for a job.

The doctor told her to eat two eggs for breakfast every day.

"Why?" asked Elizabeth, who did not like eggs.

"Greensickness," the doctor replied.

Greensickness was when a person's skin turned green because they didn't have enough iron in their blood. Eggs were full of iron, the doctor said, God's medicine. Silly old fool, said their mother, but she didn't say it to the doctor.

Whenever she passed a mirror now, Elizabeth inspected herself carefully in case she was turning green. Sometimes she thought she was, sometimes she thought she wasn't. It was one of those things, once you started looking, you could never be quite sure of. You couldn't be sure of other people either. Sometimes Elizabeth thought her mother's skin had a green look about it, or Frances's or Matilda's. Not her father's, though, or Uncle Paul's. Only women could get the greensickness, that's what the doctor said. Silly old fool, thought Elizabeth.

Now, in the middle of the night, she stood up from her bed, pulled on her sandshoes and her coat and slipped out the front door. She picked up the bucket she kept by the flowerbed, and reached into her coat pocket for her torch.

There was a sandy path that led to the beach through a stretch of dense bush. There was no one about, no one at all, it was the middle of the night and she pushed her way through, tiny branches stinging her face. But it wasn't dark, she had her torch and the light of the moon and stars and the eyes of possums glowing in the trees above her.

When at last she broke through the bush and saw the wide black opening of the world, she ran down to the edge of the water and breathed in the wind, as though she was drinking the waves, like the giant in the fairy story who drank the whole world dry. She lay down on the sand, her head to one side.

My headache is gone, she thought, all gone.

Perhaps she did fall asleep, after all. It was much later when she was finally back on the road that led home, time for the sun to come up. The sky was silver and the leaves of the gum trees were wet with little bubbles of dew. Soon the milkman would come, milk bottles clinking, and the paperboy.

She had nearly reached her own front gate, when two beams of light swung behind her and she heard an engine purring. Elizabeth turned and saw a black car pulling into the driveway of the big pale house next door. She remembered what Matilda had said at lunch, about a black car and men with umbrellas.

The car stopped at the top of the drive, and two men got out. Elizabeth stood still behind a tree, watching. Goosebumps gathered along her arms and legs in the cold sea breeze. The front door of the house opened, and one of the men went inside.

The other one stayed alone outside in the darkness and lit a cigarette. He sat on the front step, silently smoking while Elizabeth watched, just a shadow of a man and a tiny flame like a firefly, becoming brighter and dimmer and then finally disappearing.

The Sydney Morning Herald

POLICE SEARCH FOR WOMAN

POLICE ARE SEARCHING for a 27-year-old woman patient missing from the Westhaven private hospital, Evans Street, Waverley, since 7 p.m. yesterday.

The woman, who has been receiving treatment for nerves, is wearing a night-dress and blue kimono with pink spots.

Police describe her as 5 ft 3 in tall, slight build, and brown hair.

Tragic Life Story Of Man–woman

Roberta Cowell's story, the story of the Spitfire pilot who is now a woman, strikes a deep chord of sympathy.

In the second instalment of her life story, in Pix out today, Roberta Cowell discloses tragic elements of her early life.

Unable to find peace and a quiet mind in many apparently normal situations, she was driven into strange and complex emotions.

Sometimes I felt so lonely, she recalls, and tells of her marriage to a girl she had known for years.

Five

MONDAY, 12 APRIL 1954

ON MONDAY MORNING Matilda leapt out of bed and bounced down the hallway with both feet together, pretending to be a kangaroo, until she reached the laundry. She had decided to find her father's tennis racquet, which he kept next to the laundry tub with a couple of old tennis balls.

Maybe I can be a champion tennis player when I grow up, she thought.

Matilda was still feeling angry about Uncle Paul shooing away the lizard. When she was angry, she tried to fill up her mind with something else, to stop it splitting into little tiny pieces. So she decided to think about tennis. There were some big girls in sixth class at her school who had tennis lessons. She had seen them riding their bikes, in white dresses and white socks and even white shoes, with their tennis racquets strapped to the handlebars. Maybe when she was in sixth class her father would let her have tennis lessons.

She took the racquet and balls and ran out into the back yard. She stood in the middle of the grass and threw the ball high in the air and tried to hit it. The first few times she missed, the racquet was too big for her and too heavy, but she held it tight with both hands and tried again. Then she hit it once a little way and then once a long way, and she couldn't find the ball anywhere.

So she tossed up the second ball and down it came, and she held the racquet up like a frying pan, and the ball bounced down onto it. She hit it up as hard as she could.

"Oh no," said Matilda, because the ball went right over the fence to the back yard of the big house.

The fence where the two yards joined was grown over with ivy and weeds and kept upright with bits of broken stone. Matilda stood up on a slab of sandstone, and peeped through the cracks of the grey, splintering wood.

There was a man in the middle of the yard, feeding little bits of bread to a kookaburra. The man was still in his pyjamas, slippers and a blue dressing gown. He had longish grey hair and a round face and he looked strange to Matilda. He did not look like her father or the headmaster or the postman or the mad old man next door.

He was taking deep breaths in and out, in and out. He

tossed the last scraps of white to the bird, who nipped it up in a beak like snapping scissors. When the man opened his mouth, his breath was like smoke in the morning mist. He stamped his feet like a racehorse ready for the starting gun, and the kookaburra flapped away cackling into the tall trees. Then the man stamped his feet again and raised his arms in the air and swung them about.

Matilda stared. The man seemed to be listening for something. Perhaps it was the waves, rolling over the sand they couldn't see, or the morning wind in the dry leaves on the lawn. Or the koalas fighting high in eucalypts, or the sound of a motorboat somewhere very far away. Perhaps he was thinking about something someone had said, or trying to remember the words of a song. Is he praying? wondered Matilda.

"Hallo," she called out, before she knew she was going to.

The man turned around.

"Hallo," said Matilda.

The man stepped towards her, hesitantly. He seemed puzzled.

"Um," said Matilda. "Did you see my tennis ball?"

Matilda leaned over the fence as far as she could and looked up and down the big and green yard filled with plants and rockeries, not like the dandelions and rusting clothesline in their back yard.

"There!" she said in relief, and pointed.

The ball had rolled underneath a huge flowering tree, and lay among the fallen purple and white petals. The man raised one finger in the air as if to say, Ah, now I understand! He walked to the tree, picked up the ball and then came back to the fence.

"Thank you," said Matilda, although he hadn't given it to her yet.

Why didn't he say anything? Maybe he'd had his tongue cut out, like that man in the Arabian Nights. But then he made as if he was going to toss the ball to her, so she held out her hands to catch it. He threw it, just a little lob in the air over the fence, and it landed in her open palms. They smiled at each other.

"Thank you," said Matilda again, for something to say.

The man bowed slightly. He glanced back at the big house.

"Goodbye," said Matilda.

It was difficult to have a conversation when the other person didn't say anything, so she decided to stop trying. She waved at him and then hopped down from the rock so she couldn't see him any more, and ran back to the laundry, tossing the racquet and ball under the tub.

In the kitchen, Elizabeth was at the table reading the paper and her mother was standing by the sink, gazing out the window.

"You're in trouble," said Floreal.

Matilda made a face.

"Who were you talking to?" Her mother wiped her wet hands with a tea towel.

"Just the man next door," said Matilda. "In the big house."

"You mustn't talk to strangers," said her mother.

"He didn't say anything," Matilda defended herself. "Only I said things."

"Who are those people, anyway?" said their mother, to nobody in particular.

"They're spies," said Floreal.

The room was filled with the sound of the radio and butter spitting in the pan on the stove. Spies? thought Matilda, scornfully. Spies weren't real, they were only in films and comics. She sat down at the table next to Elizabeth, who shuffled along in annoyance at having to move the newspaper to make space. Their mother was cooking scrambled eggs. She did it for Elizabeth's green-sickness, but Frances and Matilda had to eat them as well.

"I'm not green," Matilda complained, holding up her pink hands. She preferred toast and jam.

"You might get green," said their mother. "When you're Elizabeth's age."

But Matilda didn't think she would ever be Elizabeth's age.

"I'd better wake up Frances," said their mother.

She put a glass of milk down on the table in front of Matilda and left the room. Matilda sipped the milk up, licking the white from her lips.

Perhaps it was just as well the man in the yard next door hadn't said anything to her. What if he had come over to the fence and asked her in for a chocolate biscuit? Would she have said yes? She knew she shouldn't, but it was hard to tell until he asked her.

Six

MONDAY, 12 APRIL 1954

FRANCES WAS ALWAYS THE LAST to wake up, the last to get dressed and eat her breakfast. She liked sleeping. It was hard for her when the sun came in the window and the night was over.

She was awake, but still in her pyjamas, sitting up in bed leaning out the window when her mother came into the room.

"Look at the cars," said Frances. She had her eiderdown draped around her shoulders, like the Queen's royal robes.

There were two cars now parked outside the big house.

They glistened. Her mother sat on the bed next to her and looked.

"They must be really rich," said Frances, screwing up her face, but her mother had left the room.

Frances pulled on her uniform, rubbed the sleep from her eyes and followed her mother out to the kitchen. Elizabeth had taken her eggs and the paper into the back yard, where she lay on the grass on her stomach kicking her legs in the air, her head bent down.

"When will Elizabeth go back to school?" asked Matilda. "It's not fair."

Their mother bit her bottom lip. When she dropped a knife on the floor, the clatter made her jump.

"Shhh," she said, pointing to the radio. "Let me hear."

Frances swallowed down her scrambled eggs in a rush. It was time to go already. Their mother gave them their sandwiches and apples in brown paper bags for lunch, vegemite for Frances, sultanas for Matilda. They kissed their mother and left the house, beginning the long winding walk up and downhill, and along a narrow dusty roadway hung over with trees and vines, which would take them at last to school.

The black cars still sat in the morning sun outside the big house.

"I wish we had a car," said Matilda.

It was a steep walk. Matilda stayed very close to Frances as they passed the block of bush with the thick tall gum trees and the grey broken rock. Ghost gums, they were called. The cowboys and Red Indians were in there, planning their attack. Matilda hid behind Frances. At least that way Frances would get shot first.

Frances paid no attention to Matilda. She was thinking about waves, how they sounded like people shouting, wanting her attention. It was too cold already to swim. Frances was glad. After school in the heat of summer, everyone headed for the beach, but Frances hated it. She was afraid of the waves, the way they never stopped coming. She didn't like getting dumped, being hit on the back and having her mouth filled with sand. Also the salt made her skin and eyes sting, and the hot sand burnt the soles of her feet.

She preferred the pool. There was a big public pool not far from the school where they went for swimming carnivals. There the water was so bright blue it was like the Garden of Eden in pictures, and you could see right through the water, down to the line of black tiled stripes on the floor. Swimming in there she felt clean and safe, like being a fish in a giant tank.

When they reached the top of the hill, they could hear the school bell ringing. The children in sixth class took it in turns to pull on the rope and make the bell toll. This week it was the turn of a boy called Geoffrey. He was a big boy, much bigger than the other boys of his age. He was famous in the school for running up when the little children had their heads bent over the bubblers and banging their faces down on the metal.

Once he had banged the head of a boy in Frances's class called John. John had glasses and his nose had started to bleed and he had wandered randomly about the playground, water and blood all over his face and his glasses cracked and falling off. Geoffrey was afraid when he saw the blood and he tore right out of the school. The headmaster had to go out to find him and bring him back. Geoffrey hadn't gone far, only to the bus stop. Perhaps he was hoping a bus might come along just in time before the headmaster did and he could have gone away down the highway to another land and no one would ever see him again, like a story.

Frances had felt sorry for Geoffrey when the headmaster dragged him back into the school by the ear, even though she hated him because he made her afraid to drink from the bubblers and some days were so hot and long. The headmaster gave Geoffrey the cane on both hands. At lunchtime under the fig tree he showed them all the red marks on his palms and the backs of his legs.

Now Geoffrey rang the bell hard all the while as the children lined up in their class groups. Frances stood in her line next to her friend Gillian. Gillian had yellow hair and red skin and a little brown mouse in her pocket. She took it out and held it up by its tail to Frances's face.

"Yoo hoo," mouthed Gillian, all breath, because they were not supposed to talk in the line.

Frances and Gillian were best friends, but they didn't like each other much. They sat next to each other at play-lunch and lunchtime and in the classroom as well. They always had, ever since kindergarten. On the first day of school, Gillian had grabbed tight hold of Frances's hand and didn't let go for hours.

Frances didn't mind being with Gillian in the playground, but she wished she didn't have to sit next to her in the classroom. When they did reading, Gillian would get angry if Frances finished the book too soon, and pinched her arm hard, or even bit her. Once she stuck the sharp end of a pencil right into Frances's knee. Frances tried to read more slowly, even reading the same page seven or eight times, but sometimes she couldn't help it – the pages seemed to turn by themselves.

"ATTEN–SHUN!"

Now all the children stood to attention, slapping their feet together.

"STAND AT EASE!"

The children put their feet apart and waited.

"Good morning, children," boomed the headmaster.

"Good morning, sir," chanted the children together.

The headmaster said some more things then and Frances tried to listen but Gillian was waving the mouse upside down by the tail in front of her face, so close she could see its tiny sharp teeth.

"Don't you like him?" said Gillian.

The mouse's little teeth were so white. They reminded Frances of Mark, a boy who used to be in their class. He had white shiny teeth with pointed ends. He sat with her under the tree at lunch sometimes, when Gillian was playing skippings. Gillian was a good skipper, she almost never got out, not even when the rope went very fast, smacking on the dark pavement, smack smack smack.

Frances and Mark used to sit and watch the skipping on the low wooden benches under the fig tree. The ground was covered with tiny brown pods fallen from the huge branches above. They pressed them into each other's skin and made patterns of stars.

Mark had black hair, dark eyes and red, red lips. He had a sleepy look about him. One day as they sat under the fig tree he said to Frances, "When I am seventeen and you are sixteen, we can get married."

"All right," agreed Frances, surprised, but thinking she might as well.

In the classroom, Mark had a desk at the back all by himself. Sometimes he actually fell asleep. One of the children would turn around and see him slumped forward, his black shiny head in his arms, and they would laugh because he snored. The teacher didn't do anything, she didn't tell him to wake up, not even to write the spelling list.

Then one day, Mark did not come back to school. The place at the back of the classroom where he used to sit and sleep remained empty. Whenever she saw the empty seat, Frances felt a terrible sort of pain, somewhere underneath her skin.

The teacher never said anything about the fact that Mark had gone, but the children did. One of the boys said he had gone to Queensland. Another boy said that he had turned into a bird. Both ideas seemed equally mysterious. Then a girl called Jeanette said, "He's got polio."

"Polio?" said Frances.

Polio was bad. They knew about polio. It was as bad as TB, maybe worse. If you had polio, you had to stay inside your house or go to hospital for weeks and weeks and not come out at all. Your family as well, they were closed up in their house like a prison. And when at last you did come out, you might have metal things strapped to your arms and legs, and you could hardly walk.

Frances had never known anyone with polio, but once, when they were in town with their mother, they had seen a little girl in a blue tartan coat struggling down the street with her parents and they heard the slow, uneven clunking of metal on the pavement. "Don't look," their mother said, "that child will never run again." Frances didn't look, but stared down fiercely at the footpath while the sound of the little girl and her metal legs faded into the distance.

That child will never run again. Could that have happened to Mark?

As they filed inside, all the children in Matilda's class were talking about the Royal Easter Show. Are you going to the Show? Are you going? When are you going? We're going tonight, tomorrow, on the weekend. Are you going to the Show?

"Of course I am," said Matilda at once.

"When?"

"We're going. We're going tomorrow night."

"We're going on Saturday."

Matilda's desk was at the very front of the classroom. She had to sit there because she couldn't hear very well. A nurse had come and tested all their ears. One by one she held up a little silver watch in the air, told them to close their eyes and asked if they could hear it ticking.

"No," said Matilda in the dark.

"What about now?" said the nurse.

"No," said Matilda.

"Now?" said the nurse.

Matilda tried hard. Could she hear it?

"I don't know," she said. "Maybe."

The nurse told the teacher and the teacher told Matilda's mother that was why Matilda couldn't read or write properly, and now she had to sit right at the front to make sure she could understand. Matilda did not like to be so near the teacher and to see her shiny skin from so close up, and smell her hairspray and lipstick. Her teacher was so clean, much cleaner than Matilda. She was glossy all over.

Now the teacher was standing by the tall window of the classroom.

"Are you going to the Show, Matilda?" asked the teacher, with a smile.

"Yes," said Matilda, looking away. She didn't like it when the teacher talked to her.

Right in front of her, in the middle of the teacher's

desk, was the all-day sucker, a huge disc of rainbow sugar covered in cellophane, the prize for the best pet at the parade tomorrow. Matilda's eyes were fixed on it. It was too much, it being so close. She could just reach out her hand and take it. She wanted it, they all wanted it. She could have won it, if she'd had the goanna. Now what could she do?

I'll think of something, thought Matilda.

Would they go to the Show? Their father, who might take them, was away. He should be home soon, though, he was coming home for Easter. Their mother wouldn't take them by herself. Maybe Uncle Paul will take us, thought Matilda, brightening…

Uncle Paul took them out sometimes. He liked going out to places. It had been Uncle Paul's idea, after all, to go to the Basin.

The Sydney Morning Herald

Dazed Girl Dragged From Water

A TUG CREW YESTERDAY dragged a semi-conscious 19-year-old girl from the water at Pyrmont a few minutes before the Orient liner Otranto sailed for London.

Police said that the girl had been farewelling a member of Otranto's crew, and when lines were being cast off the girl was asked to move away from the edge of the wharf.

A few minutes later officers on the Otranto saw the girl struggling in the water.

The crew of a nearby tug dragged her aboard, and she was treated at Sydney Hospital for shock and immersion.

Later at Central police station a 19-year-old girl was charged with having attempted to commit suicide.

She will appear before the Lunacy Court this morning.

EIGHT MORE POLIO CASES

Eight cases of poliomyelitis were reported yesterday in New South Wales, a Health Department official said last night.

He said the victims are a girl one year old, and seven boys and men from one to 23.

So far this year, 334 cases of polio, including seven deaths, have been reported in N.S.W.

In the same period last year 268 cases, including 13 deaths, were reported.

> *Tuesday*, APRIL 13, 1954 <

SIX-YEAR-OLD KATE AT THE SHOW

"Longest Morning I've Ever Spent" She Said.

SHE ATE FAIRY FLOSS, potato chips, salted peanuts and a double-header pineapple ice cream. She drank orange cordial and handed back her paper cup when she had finished. She saw the pigs, the dogs, the cows, the bulls, the woodchop.

She went twice on the slippery dip and once on a roundabout. She bought a spangled doll-on-a-stick, a skeleton with a fur skirt, a koala, a huge blue balloon and a bubble pipe. She won a blue and white plaster cocker spaniel at a sideshow and stared in amazement at a smoking jar of dry ice in water at an ice-cream stand.

From the moment we went through the turnstiles she was completely awed.

Seven

TUESDAY, 13 APRIL 1954

WHEN MATILDA WOKE UP on Tuesday morning, at once she had an idea for the Pet Parade. She didn't know where it came from. It was there in her head when she opened her eyes.

She got out of bed and tiptoed out to the kitchen. Under the sink there was a cupboard where her mother kept old boxes and cartons of biscuits and cereal. Matilda lifted a few of them up, looking for one that was just the right size.

In the end she chose a shoebox. Holding it, she went out the kitchen door, down the grassy lawn to the back corner of the yard. There was a pile of mossy bricks there that their father had been going to build a barbecue with, but he'd left it half-finished. It was the only wet place in the whole yard. Their mother said it must be because of a leaky pipe somewhere and they should get it fixed or they would run out of water altogether. But Matilda knew just what she would find there.

Snails gathered on the moist stones, covering them with silver trails, and in the morning sun it looked like the ruins of a fairy castle. Matilda got down on her knees, the box under her arm. There was a group of large, fat, damp snails, with their shells of grey and brown spirals, curling round and round like the galaxies in a special book about the universe their teacher let them look at on Friday afternoons.

Matilda pulled a snail stickily off the stone. Its feelers waved about in panic. She dropped it into the box. Then she scraped some moss from the sides of the bricks and put that in as well.

"There's your breakfast, snaily," she said.

She plucked another large one and tossed it in, and then another two. Then she found a group of little baby ones that had just been born, smaller than Corn Flakes, tiny and beautiful. She picked two of them up and put them in the box, along with some leaves and twigs.

I bet I win, thought Matilda. This is such a good idea.

Back in her bedroom, she found a lead pencil, and punched some holes in the lid of the box so her snails would have air. Then she began to write some letters on the side of the shoe box.

"What are you doing?" said Floreal.

Matilda started and the pencil broke – she had pressed too hard.

"Ay!" said Matilda. "Now look what you've made me do!"

"What is it?" asked Floreal.

"It's for the Pet Parade." Matilda held it up for him to see. "It's a snail hotel."

"A what?"

"A snail hotel," repeated Matilda impatiently. She pointed to where she had begun to write the word on the cardboard. "See?"

Matilda was only just learning to write, and she couldn't do much yet, just some of the capitals. But she could do an H and an O and a T.

"The E is back to front," commented Floreal.

"No it's not," retorted Matilda. When she frowned, her whole face seemed to cave in and her eyes became even darker. "You're just jealous."

"Snails don't have hotels, anyway," said Floreal.

Matilda didn't care what Floreal thought. It was a beautiful snail hotel. Uncle Paul lived in a hotel. Matilda wished they could go and see it. She had never been in a real hotel.

"It's not for little girls," Uncle Paul said gravely, when she asked him to take her there.

Matilda knew what that meant. It was too good for little girls, too marvellous, too wonderful. But at least her snails could have their own hotel. She lifted the lid. They sat there quietly, wet and wondering. She reached in and found one of the tiny ones hiding under a leaf. She lifted it carefully up into the air and its foot wiggled about, just like a real baby.

It was hard for Matilda and Frances to kiss their mother goodbye that morning. Matilda was holding the snail hotel in front of her and Frances had a felt flowerpot strapped on her head with a piece of elastic. Frances had worn the same flowerpot hat to the parade for the past three years. Of course she never won a prize. Frances has no ambition, Uncle Paul always said, but then Matilda has enough for all of us.

"Don't you ever want to do something different?" asked Matilda.

"No," said Frances.

"Don't you want to win a prize?"

"No," said Frances.

Their mother blew them kisses as she stood at the front door and waved goodbye. They could see the mad old man next door, glaring at them through the wire flyscreen.

"Good morning," their mother called out uneasily.

The mad old man banged his stick on the floor in reply.

"I bet I win," said Matilda to Frances, as they walked up the hill. "This is such a good idea."

She was glad to get out of the house, not only to get to school, but also she wanted to get away from Floreal and all the mean things he kept saying about her snail hotel. Floreal never followed her outside, he never came to school. She skipped forward, clutching the box to her chest.

Just then a car appeared, swooping up towards them like a magpie. It was one of the shiny black cars from the house next door. Frances and Matilda scuffled to the side of the road. The car braked and the man who was driving leant his head out, his elbow resting on the edge of the window.

"Want a lift to school, girls?" he grinned.

He reached behind him and opened the back door and it swung wide onto the road. Frances and Matilda looked at each other, and then they climbed in the back seat. Frances pushed her flowerpot to one side, to stop it hitting the roof of the car, while Matilda balanced the snail hotel on her lap. There was another man sitting in the front passenger seat. He didn't smile at all.

"Like your hat," said the driver to Frances, but she turned her head away quickly and looked out the window.

This car is so beautiful, thought Matilda. The seats were dark brown leather and smelt so new. Silver things shone all about her, ashtrays and handles. As it drove along the winding gravel road through the wilderness of trees and falling leaves, the car hardly seemed to make a noise. It was like flying.

"What've you got in the box?" said the driver to Matilda, giving up on Frances.

Matilda could see the driver's face in the rear-vision mirror. He had light blue eyes and dark eyebrows. It was strange to talk to someone back-to-front, with a face made of glass.

"Snails," she said. "It's a snail hotel."

"Is that so?" The driver shook his head in wonder. "What will they think of next?"

"Have you come to live next door?" asked Matilda.

"That's right," nodded the driver in the mirror.

"For ever?"

"Probably not," he said.

He glanced at the man in the passenger seat next to him. His arms were tightly folded in front of him, and he didn't look very pleased.

"You going to the Show this year, girls?" asked the driver, changing the subject.

"Yes," said Matilda.

Frances looked at her sideways, as if to say, that's not true.

"We are going to the Show," said Matilda defiantly. "My dad will take us. He's coming home at Easter."

They had reached the corner of the street which led to the school.

"Drop you off here, kids," said the driver.

He pulled the car over and brought it to a stop, but he didn't turn off the engine. It was like a big growling cat. Matilda tried to open the door on her side, but she couldn't do it, so the driver leaned back and opened it for her. His hands were large and there were dark hairs on his fingers, like a pirate. When he sat back in his seat he winked at her in the rear-vision mirror. Matilda laughed.

"Bye bye," she said, tumbling out, hanging onto the box.

"Thank you." Frances crawled over the leather seat and got out of the car. Her flowerpot fell halfway off her head, but she pulled it back upright as she slammed the door behind her.

Almost instantly the car took off again. It disappeared, leaving low clouds of crimson dust behind it.

"We shouldn't have done that, Matilda," said Frances. "Don't tell anyone."

"I won't," said Matilda.

Eight

TUESDAY, 13 APRIL 1954

WHEN FRANCES AND MATILDA WALKED into the playground the air was full of anxious noise, of squirming and escape. Quite apart from all the children in hats with streamers and feathers, there were dogs barking, clawing cats, guinea pigs in baskets, budgies in cages, ducks and chickens with strings on their feet, and even a goat with a rope around its neck.

Matilda searched about for a girl called Angela who had said she was going to bring a pony and Matilda had been so jealous. But there she was, with no animal at all, just wearing a straw hat with a few flowers in it.

"Can I see?" asked a boy called Philip, coming up to Matilda.

Matilda opened the lid of the box and let him look inside, and suddenly it seemed there were a hundred children crowding around and staring at it, poking their fingers, reaching in. Matilda felt a panic rise up inside her, and she thought she might scream and her face and cheeks were hot.

"ATTEN–SHUN!"

Someone had forgotten to ring the bell, there was too much excitement. But the parade was not till eleven o'clock, so they had to go into their classrooms until then. The goat was tied up near the taps so it could lick the dripping water when it was thirsty. It bleated all morning as they sat in the warm classroom, copying things down from the board about the transit of Venus. Then it became very quiet, falling asleep in the sunshine.

When at last it was time for the parade, Matilda couldn't remember what she'd been doing, only they must have been writing because her tabletop was covered with pencil shavings. She stood with her snail hotel in a line with the other children and felt as though she would faint. She couldn't eat. She gave her apple to Frederick, a boy with a large and mesmerising chickenpox scar in the middle of his forehead.

Out in the sunny playground, first to march around were the children with hats. It seemed to take forever, all those boring hats. There was Frances and her flowerpot falling off, she didn't even seem to notice. Matilda's legs wanted to run fast, as though her feet might take off without her, but she said to herself over and over again, Keep still, keep still.

Finally it was time for the Pet Parade. Now, the headmaster told them, rather than him choosing a winner, the children themselves could vote.

"Just like voting in an election," he bellowed through a hand-held megaphone. "When you children are twenty-one, you will all be able to vote."

"If you vote for my snail hotel," said Matilda urgently to Frederick, "I will give you my lunch every day this week."

"Now remember, children," continued the headmaster, "the prize is for the most unusual pet. Not the best-looking or the most obedient. The most unusual."

"I will give you an Easter egg," said Matilda to Frederick.

"So have a good look at all the candidates," said the headmaster. "Mrs Peterson will give you a piece of paper for you to write down which pet you think should win. Then you will put it in here" – he held up a wastepaper basket – "and then I will count them and announce the winner."

"What about me?" said a boy called Owen. "Do I get an Easter egg?"

"You too," said Matilda immediately.

"Now!" The headmaster cleared his throat. "Time for the Grand Parade!"

Matilda stood tall with her shoulders back and held up her hotel in front of her, tipped downward, so everyone could see the snails in their magnificent green palace. The line of competitors marched around the playground, while the other children stood in rows at the edges, shouting and clapping.

The boy with the goat went first, pulling it along with the rope, then a couple of dogs also with ropes, a cat in a box that was too frightened to get out, Frances's friend Gillian with her horrible mice that she put on top of her head so they clung to her yellow hair, then a boy with a white chicken under one arm and a sign on his hat saying "Sunday Lunch".

Then it was Matilda, with her snail hotel. Matilda could hear clapping and laughter, and she could see Frederick pointing and saying things to the other boys. Past the bell they marched, around the fig tree and then back again to the tune of the school's wooden flute band playing "The Minstrel Boy", "Men of Harlech" and "Waltzing Matilda".

Matilda felt dizzy, the sun was so hot and right above her head. She saw Mrs Peterson handing out the little pieces of paper and everyone writing things down and putting them in the basket, and the headmaster coughing and smiling, striding up and down with his stick, waving it about, the same stick he had used to hit Geoffrey with six times on each hand and six times on the backs of his legs.

The sun was so high in the sky and it was so hot, even

though it was nearly Easter. Matilda felt as though her own mind was spinning up into the sun and she couldn't hear anything.

"Matilda!" said a voice. "Where are you, Matilda?"

She couldn't even hear it, but someone pushed her forward and then the all-day sucker was placed into her hand and everyone, everyone in the whole world was looking at her and clapping and she had won, she had really won it, and the white chicken squawked and flew up onto the roof of the weather shed.

"I am in a frenzy," she said to herself, a word she had heard her mother use. "I am in a frenzy," and it was the best and most wonderful place she had ever been in all her life.

Matilda was in a frenzy the rest of lunchtime, right through the afternoon. She sat very still in class, staring hard at the place on the teacher's desk where the all-day sucker had been but now was just an empty jar that soon would fill up with scissors and pencils and paintbrushes. The all-day sucker was hers, she had won it, and it was in her satchel, hanging on the metal peg outside the classroom.

The teacher was showing them how to make a bird by folding a square of coloured paper.

"It's something they do in Japan," she said, and even Matilda knew this couldn't be true because the Japanese cut off people's heads in the war. But Matilda was in a frenzy and she felt light and crisp like a piece of glass.

It was only when the bell went at last for the end of

the day that Matilda's frenzy stopped. She went outside to the line of metal pegs, to get her satchel with the all-day sucker inside it. Her snail hotel was under her arm ready for the walk home. She strapped her satchel to her back, and then she lifted the lid of the shoebox.

"Here I am, snails," murmured Matilda.

She looked down at the snails in their hotel, moving so carefully over the twigs, so patiently across the leaves and the walls of cardboard. She looked at the shining silver trails of their journeys around and around and around, like the hands on a clock, and suddenly, she didn't know why, her frenzy stopped.

Her skin turned cold and children clattered past her down the hallway to get out of school. Inside Matilda's head the cowboys and Red Indians hid in the grey-green bush and there was the smell of the gums, and there was the gun on the table in the dark room, and the black car and the rear-vision mirror, shining and gleaming like the moon.

And then finally, and she never knew why she thought of it, she never knew at all, unless it was the leaves and the streaks of silver like water, and looking down from high above and seeing everything there was, everything, she leaned against the stone wall behind her and she remembered the Basin.

Nine

IT HAD BEEN UNCLE PAUL'S idea to go to the Basin. It was Boxing Day. Because of Christmas, their father was home from his ship for four days in a row. But he slept most of the time, like a bear in a cave.

"He's tired," their mother said, holding a finger to her lips. She wanted them to be quiet too, like little ghosts.

Uncle Paul was staying with them and he was not quiet at all. He woke up early, opening windows, banging doors, whistling to the radio. He was there because at his hotel during the holiday they had a famous piano player instead of him, and he got the week off.

"Does he play better than you?" Matilda asked. "The famous man?"

"I play better than him," said Uncle Paul. "Naturally."

Early in the morning on Boxing Day they had heard their mother cry out. Matilda came out of her bedroom to see what had happened. But it was only the newspaper.

"What happened?" said Matilda, trying to see the headline, but their mother folded the paper over.

"Nothing, nothing for you to think about," she said.

Elizabeth took the newspaper from their mother, all the big flat pages, and spread it out on the kitchen table. She told Matilda what had happened in a low voice so their mother wouldn't hear. A train travelling from Wellington to Auckland had fallen off a bridge into the river, and 166 people had been drowned. On Christmas Day.

"All those poor people," moaned their mother, who had heard anyway. "All those poor little children."

Why was her mother so upset? Then Matilda remembered that her mother's friend, Yvonne, lived in New Zealand. Maybe Yvonne had drowned with all those little children.

"Was Yvonne on the train?"

"Of course not," said their mother, calming herself. "Yvonne lives in Dunedin. That's miles away."

"It says here the Queen is very sad about the train," Elizabeth read out. "She just arrived in her boat the night before."

"That Queen's a jinx," said Uncle Paul. He was sitting on the sofa, his legs stretched out. "All's well, she turns up and bang, train in the river. She'd better get out of there."

Matilda went and sat down beside him. He pushed her onto the floor but she just climbed back on.

"Poor Queen," said Matilda.

There was a picture of the Queen on the wall in her classroom at school. Matilda didn't like to think of the Queen being sad, tears dropping out of that nice face all over her lovely yellow dress. The teacher told them that the Queen was coming to Sydney in a boat for a visit, but Matilda didn't believe it. How could a queen come to Sydney? But maybe it was true, because New Zealand was not so very far away.

"Morning," said their father, rubbing his eyes as he wandered into the room in his dressing gown.

It was eight o'clock. When he was home, their father always listened to the eight o'clock news. He went over to the radio and switched it on.

"Shhh!" he waved at them.

"Don't listen," said their mother. "It'll upset you. Don't listen."

But he was already hunched over the radio, his head bent. There was a soft fanfare of music, then all the news about all the dead people, all the little children drowned in the bottom of the river, came out of the soft black space in the newsreader's placid voice. Matilda saw her father's shoulders sag and his hands began to shake. He doesn't like dead people, thought Matilda, remembering, he doesn't like them at all. Because of the war, that's what everyone said.

"I know," said Uncle Paul, standing up loud and tall.

"Let's go on a picnic! How about it? Let's go to the Basin."

The Basin was a bay not far from where they lived. Rich people went with their own boats, but other people took the ferry from the wharf at Palm Beach. Matilda and Frances had been there for school trips. There was a small, lapping lagoon for swimming and a green park for making barbecues and playing cricket, and there was a high hill of bush where Matilda had once seen a waratah flower, like a huge, bright red spider sitting on a stalk. Her teacher had taken a photograph with all the children crowded around it, as though it was a film star they had accidentally come upon, hiding in the gum trees.

"Where's Frances?" said Uncle Paul. "Where's my friend Frank? Go and wake her up."

"What's high treason?" asked Elizabeth, from under the newspaper.

Their father switched off the news and all the little men inside closed their mouths at once.

"In Russia some people have been shot by a firing squad for high treason," said Elizabeth. "It says they betrayed the Motherland."

"There you are, then," said Uncle Paul.

"Who got shot?" asked Matilda.

"A man called Beria and six other people," read Elizabeth, pondering. "It says they were 'reptiles in human masks'."

"Yuck," said Matilda.

"Oh, stop it!" snapped their mother, and she snatched the paper away from Elizabeth and squeezed it out of sight behind the bread bin. Their father had gone out into the garden, the screen door swinging shut behind him.

"Come on, girls!" said Uncle Paul, clapping his hands together. "What about our picnic?"

They were going to the Basin! Matilda got dressed quickly, with her swimsuit underneath her shorts. She pushed Frances hard, and told her what was happening. Frances grimaced, but she got out of bed.

Out in the kitchen, their mother was wrapping up pieces of bread, and talking about sausages and steak, how they would build a fire and stay until sunset and take the last ferry back to Palm Beach. Out in the back yard their father was pacing up and down.

"What's wrong with Daddy?" asked Matilda.

"He'll be all right," said their mother. "It's just his nerves. He'll come in."

"Do not forsake me, oh my darling," sang Uncle Paul.

He was wearing a singlet so you could see his sunburnt arms and his tattoo of an elephant.

"It's so I don't forget you," he explained to Matilda. "Elephants never forget."

Matilda knew the story, the elephant who remembered the people who teased him when he was young, finally killing them years and years afterwards.

"Can you really remember things that long?" asked Matilda.

"He's a man, not an elephant," their mother said. "Men are different. They forget."

"On this our wedding day," sang Uncle Paul.

Well, men were different, even Matilda could see that. Their mother's skin was white as clouds and she didn't have a tattoo and she always smelt so clean and her fingernails were smooth and pale pink. But you never knew what she was thinking.

"I've got such a headache," she said that morning, biting her bottom lip, and she took a powder with a glass of water.

Their father came inside, and was in the laundry cleaning out the picnic basket. Elizabeth found a blanket for them to sit on, an old tartan blanket from the bottom of her wardrobe. Even Frances was ready, and had finished her toast.

"Let's go," said Uncle Paul cheerfully. "Let's hit the water."

They set off from the house, laden with bags and hats. Matilda had a big spade under her arm and a bucket for digging. She was planning on building an elaborate giant castle in a secret place away from everyone else, where she wouldn't be disturbed. She raced ahead of them all. Their father quickened his step, leaving the others behind.

"Wait, Matilda!" called out their mother.

She always wants to be first, thought Frances, in everything. She had a tennis ball and was bouncing it as they walked. Uncle Paul kept trying to snatch it from her.

But Matilda ran ahead not because she wanted to be first but because she wanted to get past the place where the cowboys and Red Indians were hiding. If she rushed past, they wouldn't have time to shoot at her. They would be sitting round the campfire and hear her footsteps, but by the time they looked through the gum leaves she would be gone.

Their mother was wearing her red shoes with the gold buckles, click click as she walked.

"It's a picnic," said Uncle Paul reprovingly. "You'll ruin those lovely shoes."

But their mother just smiled faintly. It was a warm day, no wind, no clouds, just sun and sun and sun. Their mother covered her white arms with a pale pink cotton shawl with little butterflies embroidered on it. Their father had brought it back from India. He had sailed on a boat all the way to India, it was hard to believe. But in the war he had sailed even further; he said, India is only halfway for me.

Uncle Paul was still singing.

"I'm not afraid of death, but oh!
What will I do if you leave me?"

By the time they reached the wharf there was quite a crowd of people waiting and they could see the ferry chugging over.

"We'll miss it! We'll miss it!" cried their mother anxiously. "Come on!"

Their father broke into a run, taking long heavy strides, holding the picnic basket close to him with his big arms. But the ferry was slow and it creaked and swung from side to side on the rolling water and their hats blew off and Matilda found herself pushed aside in the crowd and she squeezed up against a blind man with dark glasses and a white stick and one of his front teeth was missing.

"Pardon me," he said, reaching out his hand.

Matilda felt her heart beating under her swimsuit that was too tight even though it was nearly new and her mother would be cross. I can't help growing, thought Matilda, I'd stop it if I could.

Once on the ferry she was wedged in by people and bags of meat and bottles of beer and lit cigarettes and she thought she could hear her mother's voice but she couldn't be sure and anyway she couldn't move. The blind man had found a place to sit down and he was smiling to himself. It's like the opposite of being invisible, thought Matilda. Everyone can see him, but he can't see anyone else.

She heard the sounds of the ferry casting off, the pulling in of the wooden gangplank, the low hooting, the grind of the engine, the splash of the rope as it fell in the water, to be pulled in dripping by the deckhand. They were leaving, all of them, leaving the world.

"There you are, you monkey!"

Matilda turned. There was Uncle Paul, pushing his way through.

"Your mum thinks you fell overboard," he said, beckoning. "Come and show her you're alive and well."

But if her mother had thought that, she must have already forgotten because when Matilda followed Uncle Paul to the outside deck of the ferry, her mother was sitting next to their father, holding his hand, wordlessly looking out at the ocean.

"Found her," said Uncle Paul and he lit a cigarette.

Matilda searched the deck for Elizabeth and Frances. They were at the very front of the ferry, their legs hanging over the edge. Frances had put her tennis ball in her pocket and it bulged. Elizabeth's hair was tangling in the wind.

"Daddy looks funny," said Matilda, squeezing herself between them.

"I think it was the news," said Elizabeth. "You know how he goes funny about things like that."

"He doesn't like dead people," agreed Frances.

They gazed down, the three of them, at the iron-grey waves streaming swiftly under the arrowhead of the boat. The closer you looked, the faster it seemed, but it's just an illusion, said Elizabeth, it just looks like that.

"Row, row, row," thought Matilda, remembering the Argonauts, the jolly-band-of-rowers, row, row, row.

Now the ferry was almost quiet, the engine had died down. They felt the whole ocean rocking beneath them. Pressed in between Elizabeth and Frances's warm legs, Matilda was safe, but she knew that under the sleek surface lay mysterious things, sharks and stingrays and even submarines, Germans and Japanese.

You wouldn't know they were there, their father told them, all those men under there, all of them locked up in a sub, just like you, waiting for the end. You only knew because of the radar, ping, ping, ping. The sound of a bell-bird in the bush, their father said. In the war that's all I heard all day and all night, he said, ping, ping, ping. It can drive you out of your mind, he said, that sound.

"The ocean is strong and very deep," said Elizabeth, "but nothing is as strong as the H-Bomb."

Frances looked up.

"What's the H-Bomb?" asked Matilda.

Elizabeth knew all about the H-Bomb. She had read about it in the newspaper.

"It can destroy the world in a single second," she said, and her voice was dreamy. "All life will just go phhht. Imagine that," said Elizabeth to Matilda and Frances. "Everything gone, just like that. It'll all be empty, for ever and ever."

"Do not forsake me, oh my darling," hummed Uncle Paul behind them, while the smoke from his cigarette flew up in the wind.

Matilda felt afraid but Elizabeth shook her head gently. She touched Matilda's hand.

"You don't have to be frightened," she said. "You won't even know it's happened. It'll just go bang. You won't know anything about it at all. It's only knowing things that makes you afraid," said Elizabeth, as the ferry left the world behind and sped towards the Basin.

The Sydney Morning Herald

> *Wednesday*, APRIL 14, 1954 <

RUSSIAN SPY RING IN AUSTRALIA

SOVIET DIPLOMAT IN CANBERRA REVEALS DETAILS

Mr. Menzies Promises Full Judicial Inquiry

CANBERRA, Tuesday.— Mr. V. M. Petrov, Third Secretary of the Russian Embassy to Canberra and agent of the Russian secret police (M.V.D.) in Australia, has forsaken his Russian allegiance and been granted political asylum in Australia.

> *Wednesday*, APRIL 14, 1954 <

Petrov "Salted Away": Security Screen

CANBERRA, Tuesday.— A strict and inflexible security screen has been clamped down on all personal particulars of Petrov.

It is understood that not even the Prime Minister knows his whereabouts.

A high authority said to-night: "Petrov has been salted away and he must be kept alive. The less that is said about him at present the safer it will be."

Acquaintances describe Petrov as short and dark with a more "European-looking" face than many other Soviet diplomats. He speaks English haltingly and is quick to smile.

As a secret police official, he mixed informally with Canberra people, unlike other Russian diplomats. He was often seen drinking in hotel bars.

The Sydney Morning Herald

Wife Will Go Back

CANBERRA,
Tuesday.— Mr. Petrov's wife did not seek asylum in Australia with him and she elected to remain with the Russian Embassy, where she is a stenographer.

It was learned to-night that she will return to Russia soon.

Alsatian Dog

A neighbour said he did not know Mr. Petrov, but had often seen him walking along the street with an Alsatian dog.

Tonight there was no sign of the dog at No. 7 Lockyer Street.

People living in the house on the other side of Mr. Petrov's house would not come to the door when the reporter rang the door bell.

Through a closed glass door, a woman said: "We haven't had anything to do with the Russians and we don't know anything about them".

Ten

ON WEDNESDAY MORNING, the day after the Pet Parade, Frances was snoring, but Matilda was awake early again. The all-day sucker, her wonderful prize for the snail hotel, lay on the floor beneath her bed. She'd put it under her pillow at first, but the cellophane crackled whenever she turned her head, so she pushed it away and it fell down the side of the bed with a thump onto the floor.

She hadn't shown it to anyone, not her mother, not Elizabeth, not even Frances. No one knew she had won it, except Frances, and Frances wouldn't say anything. That was a good thing about Frances. If she thought it was strange, she still wouldn't say anything.

Matilda didn't know why, but it made her feel sick to look at the lollipop now it was hers, the multicoloured swirling disc the size of a baby's face, like a little moon in her hands on the end of a stick. She didn't want to talk about it or even see it.

As for the snail hotel, that was worse. As soon as she'd got home from school, she hid it at the back of some bushes near the front fence. She left it there with the lid off so the snails could escape and go back to their normal snail life. They could all crawl away, leaving long silver trails and wondering what had happened to them.

"Why won't you show it to anyone?" said Floreal, right in her ear. "Why not?"

Matilda put her hands over her ears. Shut up, she thought, shutup shutup. None of your business! she wanted to shout. What do you care? She dashed out into the back yard. She felt restless as an insect, she wanted to rush around in circles until she was too tired to think any more.

Then she heard voices, low murmurs and a laugh.

Matilda stopped running and rolled in a somersault down to the falling-down fence. She raised herself on her elbows and peered through to the back yard of the big house.

The two men who had given her and Frances a lift in the car the day before were out there under the lemon tree, smoking. Mr Driver and Mr Passenger, Matilda thought. She climbed up on the lump of crumbling sandstone and leaned over the fence and said, "Hallo!"

The men looked up. They seemed very surprised. Perhaps they had forgotten her.

"It's me," said Matilda.

"Hallo there," replied Mr Driver, walking over, his cigarette pointing down at the ground. "It's the snail girl."

"Hallo," replied Matilda. She hung her arms over the wooden palings.

"How are you this morning?" said Mr Driver.

Matilda shrugged. She was all right. It was funny seeing his face straight on, and not in the mirror.

"Do you want to see a trick?" he asked.

"Yes," said Matilda.

Mr Driver put his cigarette up to his mouth and breathed in, pursing up his lips. When he breathed out he made a smoke ring, a luminous grey fading circle, and then another, disappearing up into the wide blue sky, one after the other.

Matilda clapped her hands, impressed.

"How do you do that?"

"I'll teach you when you're bigger," said Mr Driver, winking at Mr Passenger.

There was a pause.

"Is the other man coming out soon?" asked Matilda conversationally.

No one spoke. The only sound was the waves, rolling over the surface of the ocean. Matilda had an odd feeling, as though she was in trouble. When she was in trouble, she kept quiet.

"What other man?" said Mr Passenger carefully.

Matilda hadn't heard his voice before. She didn't like the sound of it.

"Matilda!"

It was her mother, tapping on the half-open kitchen window at her. Even at that distance, Matilda could hear a kind of frown in her voice.

"You'd better go," said Mr Driver, drawing again on his cigarette. "Don't keep Mum waiting."

"You shouldn't talk to strangers, you know," her mother said, shaking her head at Matilda as she came inside, the screen door banging behind her.

"They're not strangers," Matilda defended herself. "They're neighbours."

"You're too friendly for your own good," sighed her mother, putting a plate of two eggs on the table in front of her. "That's going to get you in trouble one day."

Well, that's silly, thought Matilda. She stared down at the eggs, like two huge moist yellow eyes. How can you be too friendly? Be a good friend to everyone, that's what my teacher says, every living thing. Every Living Thing.

I want to be friends with everything, thought Matilda, her head rushing, not just living things. I want to be friends even with stones and houses and big blocks of wood and glass. I can be friends with whoever I like, even the men next door.

The Sydney Morning Herald

"He Is Kidnapped," Says Petrov's Wife

CANBERRA, Wednesday — Mrs. Petrov, her eyes red from crying, said to-day that she did not believe her husband, the former Third Secretary at the Soviet Embassy in Canberra, had sought Australian asylum.

"I think he is kidnapped," she said.

Mrs. Petrov, a small attractive blonde woman, was being interviewed at the Soviet Embassy in Canberra, with the consent of the Soviet Ambassador, Mr. N. I. Generalov.

"QUIET COUPLE"

The neighbours described the Petrovs as a "quiet couple who never interfered with us in any way."

One said: "We saw very little of them. They almost invariably left the house about 8.30 a.m., and were not seen for the rest of the day.

"I assume they went to the Embassy which is only about 300 yards away.

"Mrs. Petrov is always very smart and well-dressed."

Another Russian couple has been living in the Petrovs' comfortable, unpretentious house since Petrov disappeared nearly a fortnight ago.

But to-day the house was deserted. There were suitcases and pieces of clothing in the lounge-room, but no sign of life.

The Petrovs' savage Alsatian dog, which terrified some of the neighbours, had also disappeared. A boy said he had seen the dog roaming the streets since the Petrovs left.

The Sydney Morning Herald

> *Thursday*, APRIL 15, 1954 <

POLICE ISSUE WARNING ON FIREARMS

POLICE YESTERDAY warned holidaymakers against the unlawful use of firearms during the holiday weekend.

The Metropolitan Police Superintendent Mr. W.F. Salmon said: 'Police authorities again warn the public against unauthorised shooting.

"It is an offence to carry or use firearms on a Sunday.

"If it is desired to shoot on private property permission of the landholder must first be obtained."

Eleven

THURSDAY, 15 APRIL 1954

ON THURSDAY, SCHOOL BROKE UP for the Easter holidays. They heard footsteps coming up the front path.

"Daddy?" said Matilda, jumping up.

They were expecting their father to come home from his ship, he should be home already. Their mother ran to open the front door. But it was Uncle Paul.

She threw herself in his arms, thought Elizabeth, watching them. In books people were always throwing themselves in each other's arms, and perhaps in real life as well.

"Don't you have to play the piano today?" she asked.

"Don't I deserve a day off?" rejoined Uncle Paul cheerfully.

"Can you take us to the Show?" said Matilda.

"Ah, the Show, the Show," groaned Uncle Paul, flopping on the sofa, "always the Show."

"Can you?" said Matilda.

"He won't," said Floreal.

Go away, thought Matilda, just go away. She kicked out her leg, trying to get at Floreal, but because he was invisible she missed, and stubbed her toe on the floor instead.

"Let's have fish and chips for tea," said Uncle Paul to their mother. "What do you say?"

Could they?

"What do you say, my friend Frank?"

Uncle Paul leant over to Frances, who was sitting quietly chewing on her nails. He poked her in the stomach. Uncle Paul liked to tease Frances, trying to make her laugh. Frances is so sad and solemn, he said. She should work for an undertaker.

"All right," mumbled Frances.

They walked down together to the fish-and-chip shop, which was opposite a little beach where the shops were. It was cold and getting dark, but Uncle Paul bought lots of fish and chips wrapped up in newspaper and handed them each a packet to hold to their chests, like a hot water bottle.

They went and sat on some wooden seats across the road to eat them. Salt and heat and oil rose in the dim air. Soon they were surrounded by red-eyed seagulls.

"Don't feed them, Mattie," warned their mother. "It's not good for them."

"It's fish," replied Matilda, throwing a big piece in the middle of the flock so they squawked and fought over it as though they hadn't eaten in weeks. "Fish is what they eat."

"It's not fish really," said Elizabeth. "It's shark."

Matilda licked the salt from her lips. Shark. Once they had been at the beach when a shark had come. No one saw the sharp grey fin rising above the ocean, but a siren went off and they all had to get out from the water and wait for it to go away. Their father had bought them each a lemonade iceblock to eat while they waited. Then he had lain on his back in the sun, his eyes closed tightly, his arms and legs stretched out on the sand.

"We'll have cooked daddy for dinner," their mother joked, but actually they'd had fish and chips that day as well.

"It's not fish really," their father told them. "It's shark."

"Yuck," said Matilda.

"It's the best," he grinned. "No bones."

It seemed a long time ago. Now their father was away on his ship when he should be at home. Matilda stood at the water's edge, where little waves lapped over her sandals as the sun was setting. Her mouth was dry and salty and there was shark inside her.

She stared out across the bay, over towards the high dark bush where the Basin was, a mountainous shape in the twilight. I thought no one could get me up there,

Matilda remembered, high in the highest branch of the tallest tree.

It was a secret that she had climbed that tree. She wasn't allowed to climb trees that high. She might tumble down and crack her head open and her brains would fall out. That happened to her mother's friend Yvonne's little brother when he was only three and Yvonne had never got over it, never. Why didn't they put his brains back in? asked Matilda and her mother said, You silly goose, once your brains fall out that's it, it's all over. So they left his brains on the street and Yvonne never got over it.

Matilda didn't care about Yvonne's little brother and it wasn't a tree he fell out of, it was a truck. She climbed the tree that day in secret when no one was looking, higher than she had ever climbed before. How high she was, so high you could see everything, like a bird in the blue sky, she could see the whole of the Basin.

I am such a good climber, Matilda thought, but in fact she nearly fell, down from the top of the tallest tree in the world. Her foot had slipped and she was going to fall, she was, she really was, down down down to the dead earth, but just in time she thought of Yvonne's little brother and his brains all over the street, and she had grabbed the branch above her head and gripped it so hard her hand bled.

Now, on the little beach where they ate their fish and chips, a flock of cockatoos rose up in the sunset from the trees, cawing, with their golden crests shining and their white, white wings spread wide. For a moment the world swayed in front of her and she felt her arms and legs begin to tremble.

"But I don't want to remember," said Matilda out loud.

And she closed her eyes tightly, so very tightly, just like her father on his back on the sand when the shark came.

The Sydney Morning Herald

"LUDICROUS" SAYS MENZIES

Declaring that the suggestion that Petrov had been kidnapped was "ludicrous", Mr. Menzies said he knew what the Communist propaganda line would be.

"The next thing they"ll be saying is that we are using drugs on Petrov," he said.

"We don't go in for that kind of thing (kidnapping) in Australia."

BIRDS TORMENTED BY SHOW CROWDS

Barricades erected at the Show to protect pheasants were useless, exhibitors claimed yesterday.

Birds have been tormented by people poking sticks into the cages and by women pulling out their feathers.

A prize bird suffered a cerebral hemorrhage yesterday and is expected to die within a few days.

Exhibitors think the injury was caused by people poking sticks into the cage.

This caused the pheasant to flap up and down, bashing its head on the tin sides of the cage.

Twelve

ON FRIDAY THERE WAS NO SCHOOL. Their mother toasted hot-cross buns on the grill, lifting them up with a fork to see how brown they were.

They all ate them, even Uncle Paul. He was greedy like a child. Matilda liked that. She hated the way grown-ups always said, That's enough, thank you, no, I really can't manage any more, how they wiped their mouths and cast their eyes downward. Uncle Paul was greedy, he never said no and he always wanted more.

"What's that ghastly music?" he said, kicking the back door open with a plate in one hand, a hot-cross bun in the other.

They listened. It was coming from the big house next door. It was as though the house was singing, deep, long, dreary notes.

"Who are those people, anyway?" Uncle Paul raised his hands in the air theatrically. "Sounds like a death march."

He let the door swing shut, and went and sat at the piano. He licked his fingers one by one because they were covered in butter, then he began to play a tune on the high-up notes.

"That certain night, the night we met,
There was magic abroad in the air!"

sang Uncle Paul. Matilda slid herself next to him on the piano stool.

"Are you going to church at Easter?"

"Are you?" replied Uncle Paul.

"I don't know," said Matilda.

"There were angels dining at the Ritz
And a nightingale sang in Berkeley Square."

Uncle Paul was playing the very top notes so softly he had to bend his ear down to the keys to hear it.

"I may be right, I may be wrong,
But I'm perfectly willing to swear
That when you turned and smiled at me —"

"Can we go to the Show today?" asked Matilda.
"A nightingale sang in Berkeley Square!"

"You're not supposed to go to the Show on Good Friday," said their mother.

"Why not?" frowned Matilda.

"God doesn't like it, darling," said Uncle Paul with a wink. "Don't they teach you anything at school?" He tugged at Matilda's bare feet and shivered. "Ice blocks," he said. "How can you stand it?"

"Daddy likes the Show," sniffed Matilda. "He'll take us. When's he coming?"

"Soon, soon," said their mother. "Blow your nose, Matilda. Get a hankie."

Matilda rolled off the piano stool and lay down on the floor, gazing at the ceiling. If you looked long enough, it started to seem as if it was coming down on top of you, closer, closer, closer, until you felt you were going to be squashed to death underneath it. Then you jumped up and escaped just in time.

"The streets of town were paved with gold
It was such a romantic affair,
And when you turned and smiled at me
A nightingale sang in Berkeley Square!"

Uncle Paul stopped playing. He breathed out heavily.

"What a pity, what a pity!" Uncle Paul twirled his grey moustache.

"What's a pity?" asked Matilda, sitting up.

"That life's not like that," said Uncle Paul. "What a pity it is."

On top of the piano was the photograph of their mother and father at their wedding, and their mother's friend Yvonne. Now Yvonne was a thousand miles away in New Zealand, but when Uncle Paul raised his eyebrows at her, it seemed to Matilda as though Yvonne raised hers back at him. But she couldn't have, of course, she was only a photo. A photo was not alive, it couldn't move. But maybe it was like a zombie, a dead person that's really alive, like Yvonne's dead-alive husband in the Solomon Islands.

"Where's Berkeley Square, anyway?" she asked, not wanting to think about zombies.

Uncle Paul swung around on the piano stool.

"It's nowhere," he said glumly. "It doesn't exist."

"Yes it does," said Elizabeth. She looked over from the sofa, where she was reading the paper. "It's in London. In England."

"How do you know?" said Matilda.

"It's nowhere," repeated Uncle Paul.

Nowhere, nowhere, nowhere. London was so far away, it might as well be nowhere. Uncle Paul smiled at their mother. The room smelt of burnt bread. Their mother pushed her hair back from her brow. She had soft swinging hair, she washed it in Lux soap.

"Perfect hair," said Uncle Paul, as he let his fingers fall lightly on the keys. "Your mother has perfect hair."

He reached over and took a handful of her hair and held it up to the sunlight, strands slowly falling down onto her shoulders.

"He shouldn't be here," said Floreal. "He shouldn't be here, when your father's away."

Matilda ran out into the back yard. The music coming from the big house next door had stopped and it was almost quiet now. But she could hear something else, someone coughing. Who was it?

She remembered what Floreal had said, how the men next door were spies. Could they be spies? Who were they spying on? Maybe I could be a spy, thought Matilda suddenly. I could watch them, without them knowing I'm here.

She lay down on her stomach and pulled herself along the grass with her arms and wiggled like a snake, right up to the crack in the fence. Then she looked through the splintered wood.

There he was again, the funny-looking man who had thrown her back the tennis ball. He was quite close to her, sitting at the garden table, laying out a chess set on a chequered board. Carefully, one by one, he was putting the pieces in their places, the little horses and little castles, the queen with a crown and the king with a cross, half of them black, half of them white, the bishops, and the pawns.

Who's he going to play with? wondered Matilda.

Bang bang went the back door. Matilda put her hands up to her eyes in the shape of binoculars and looked through. They were men, but not the men that had given her and Frances the lift. Why were there so many men? How many people can you have in one house?

One of them came and stood next to the table, looking at the chess set, and muttering something Matilda couldn't hear. There was a burst of laughter, but her man, the tennisball man, didn't smile. He rubbed his head as though he had a headache.

He'd probably like a hot-cross bun, thought Matilda.

But she kept her mouth firmly shut. She didn't want them to know she was there, not this time. She kept absolutely quiet, softer than a snail. She even tried not to breathe. After all, she was a spy.

> *Saturday*, APRIL 17, 1954 <

Russian Easter

CANBERRA, Friday.— Vladimir Petrov is reported to be having a traditional Russian Easter in his Australian security hide-out.

A Canberra source said to-night that records of Russian Easter music had been sent there for him.

Between sessions of dictating information to be used in the Royal Commission on espionage, Petrov is also listening to the radio.

He is interested in the news sessions describing developments since he fled the Russian Embassy a fortnight ago.

> *Saturday*, APRIL 17, 1954 <

GOOD FRIDAY IN SYDNEY — A CHURCH PROTEST, THE SHOW AND A CIRCUS

AFFIRMING THAT the day is not a holiday, banners in the Anglican Procession of Witness from the Domain to St Andrew's Cathedral yesterday protested against the Royal Show being open on Good Friday. An annual Good Friday event is the free performance and a distribution of buns for children by Wirth's Circus.

Thirteen

EASTER SATURDAY, 17 APRIL 1954

ON SATURDAY THEY LAY AROUND the house in a heap. Their mother sat by the telephone, dialling and dialling. She was trying to speak to their father, but she couldn't find him. At last she put the phone down.

"Let's go out!" said Uncle Paul in a loud voice, looking around at them all. "Let's go to the pictures, all the way into town, all of us."

Into town?

"But I want to go to the Show," said Matilda.

Uncle Paul rubbed her forearm up and down, shaking his head.

"The Show's too expensive, Mattie," he said. "Come on, let's take your mother to the pictures."

"If Daddy was here, we'd go," muttered Matilda.

"I'll get you an icecream," coaxed Uncle Paul.

"Can we see your hotel?" said Matilda, thinking about it, because Uncle Paul's hotel was in town.

"If you're good," replied Uncle Paul easily. "We can see a hundred hotels if you like."

But Matilda only wanted to see Uncle Paul's hotel.

"What films are on, Elizabeth?" asked their mother, and Uncle Paul smiled then, because that meant she wanted to go. "In town?"

Elizabeth folded the big thin pages over, until she found the right spot.

"We can see *Roman Holiday*," she said, "if we get a bus straight away. Or *The Robe*."

Matilda's teacher had seen *The Robe*. It was all about God. It sounded boring.

"I don't want to see that," she said. "I want to see cartoons."

"There's always cartoons, stupid," said Floreal and Matilda scowled at where she thought he was.

"It stars Gregory Peck," Elizabeth read aloud from the paper. "And Audrey Hepburn. She won an Academy Award."

"Who's Gregory Peck?" said Matilda. "I don't like him."

"He's a famous actor, darling," said their mother. "From America."

"I don't like him." Matilda was firm.

"Go and get dressed, darling," said their mother. "Tell Frances."

"On the double," added Uncle Paul.

Going to town was special, so they wore their best dresses. Matilda and Frances had exactly the same yellow-flowered dress, except that Frances's was bigger. Their father had brought them home one time from his boat. He would have brought one for Elizabeth, too, but he didn't know what size she was, so instead he got her a rectangular prism made of glass, with a little orange fish inside it. It's a paperweight, he explained, it stops all your papers flying away in the wind. But Elizabeth never opened the window so she didn't have any wind. It doesn't matter, Elizabeth told Matilda. Things don't have to be what other people say they are.

"Everybody ready?" sang out Uncle Paul.

They were ready, even Frances, all dressed up. Elizabeth wore a green skirt and shirt, Uncle Paul was in a jacket and tie and their mother stood beside him at the doorway in a beautiful pink-striped dress and brown sandals.

"She wishes she could wear her red shoes," said Floreal.

Matilda stood very still and she felt her heart beating hard. Soon she would not have to listen to him, she would be outside and the door would slam and he would be locked up in the house.

"Let's go!" she shouted. "Let's go!"

Because they lived at the ends of the earth deep in the

bush, and theirs was almost the very first stop, the bus to the city was empty. It was a double-decker and they all ran on, one after the other, up the little winding dirty staircase to the top floor. Matilda and Frances sat at the front of the bus in their yellow daisy dresses. They were so high, above all the trees and the beach and the roofs of the houses, the sloping tiles and tin and the heads of people and the tops of cars.

It was a long, long ride, away from home, through so many suburbs they hardly knew. How can there be so many people in the world, thought Matilda, there's too many. As the bus stopped and started more people got on and clambered up the stairs. Someone sat right behind Matilda and Frances, eating a pie, and Matilda was so hungry suddenly. But you couldn't ask strangers for food, although you could if it was the war and you were starving to death, their father said. The war was different, people did anything to survive, he told them. They killed each other, just to keep living. You shouldn't say things like that in front of the girls, said their mother. All right, their father said, I won't say anything.

The bus conductor was making his way down the aisle, taking money for tickets. Uncle Paul paid for them all. He had paper money. He was rich.

He's rich because he doesn't have any children, their father said. Of course he doesn't have any children, said Matilda, he's not married. It's not natural, said their father, a man should be married and have children. Oh, I'm unnatural all right, Uncle Paul agreed, quite happily.

When at last it was time to get off the bus, Matilda and Frances nearly didn't make it. They weren't quick enough coming down the winding little staircase.

"Wait!" cried Matilda. "Wait for us!"

She could not see Uncle Paul or her mother's pink dress or Elizabeth's plaited hair. Wait, please wait, don't leave us behind, and she remembered little Karen with her wooden feet and her eyes filled with tears. They were going to be left behind! But the bus waited and Uncle Paul and their mother and Elizabeth were all there on the pavement as Frances and Matilda tumbled off the last step.

"What a sausage you are, Mattie," said Uncle Paul, tugging her hair. "What's there to cry about? Look at Frances, she's not crying." He took out a big blue man's handkerchief and wiped her face dry.

"I need to go to the toilet," said Matilda.

"There's a Ladies at the cinema," suggested their mother. "Let's get there first, shall we?"

Matilda scrunched up the handkerchief and gave it back to Uncle Paul.

"Keep it," he grinned, shaking his head. "In case you want to cry in the film."

"Is it a sad story?" she asked, running to stay next to him, he was walking so fast with such big strides.

"Films are always sad," replied Uncle Paul gravely, his hair flopping over his forehead. "That's what they're for. To make you cry, like songs."

The girls hardly ever came to town. Town had its own smell, sweet and rich, and there was such a sound of footsteps, of heels on the pavements. Town was made of glass and stone and it shone. Town was hot.

"Here we are," said Uncle Paul, stopping short.

"Is this it?" breathed Matilda, gazing up. "Is that really it?"

"They've never been to the State before," said their mother to Uncle Paul.

She meant the State Theatre, that's what it was called. Even Elizabeth stared. It was a palace. It had golden gates and inside they saw chandeliers and golden-robed statues nestling in the walls, lit from behind by an orange glow like a dying fire. In large letters on the front awning they read, ROMAN HOLIDAY.

"Don't just stand there, ducklings," said Uncle Paul. "Come on in."

"Are we allowed?" asked Matilda doubtfully.

They stepped through the wide doorway. People were gathered in little groups about the room as though they were at a party. Uncle Paul marched off confidently to the queue for tickets. The girls and their mother huddled together, next to a statue of a Roman senator with a sharp nose and blank eyes. Their mother took out a lipstick and a tiny mirror from her handbag and rubbed it over her lips.

Matilda looked nervously at the shiny tiled floor. Children shouldn't be allowed in a place like this. It was too good for children. There was too much gold, too many nice chairs to sit on, it was too beautiful for them. Up high above them hung a huge chandelier, hundreds of drops of glass. It made her dizzy, just looking at it. It's like a spell, she thought, like a magic mirror broken up into pieces. It looks like ice that never melts.

Uncle Paul came back with the tickets. He gave one each to Elizabeth, Frances and Matilda.

"All in a row," he said. "Right at the front, that's all that was left."

"But what about you?" asked Elizabeth, frowning. "Where will you sit?"

"No room for us," said Uncle Paul lightly. "That's all right. I'll take your mother for a drink."

Matilda didn't understand.

"Aren't you going to see the film?"

"We'll come along afterwards," said Uncle Paul. "You'll be all right, just go in and sit down."

He reached into his pocket, took out a coin and pressed it into Elizabeth's hand.

"Buy yourselves an icecream," he said. "And don't cry too much. It's only a paper moon."

Then he and their mother were gone. It happened as instantly as a magic trick. They disappeared out of the cool golden palace, into the heat and mystery of town.

Fourteen

EASTER SATURDAY, 17 APRIL 1954

A LADY IN A RED UNIFORM stood beckoning with a torch at the curtained entrance to the stalls. Elizabeth, Frances and Matilda followed her bobbing light, down into the dark carpeted theatre. Everyone was standing up because the National Anthem was playing, "God Save the Queen".

"There you go, girls," said the lady, briefly lighting up their three seats, then she stepped away into shadows.

BANG BANG BANG BANG. The anthem was coming to an end. How loud the drum is, thought Matilda, as they felt for their seats, it must be as big as a house. Imagine the headache she must get listening to that all the time.

Because they were right in the front row, they had to lean backwards to see the screen properly. Matilda was glad the Queen was in her crown and a fur cape. She had been disappointed when the Queen came to Sydney because she'd expected her to ride the streets sidesaddle on a beautiful white horse, but instead she had sat in a big black car, waving her tiny hands wrapped up in white gloves. Nobody was allowed to touch her or she might crumble into dust.

The anthem was over now, they could sit down. The chairs were soft and springy, it was like sitting on darkness. Elizabeth bought some icecreams from a boy with a basket standing in the aisle and she passed a brick of vanilla to each of them.

Matilda started to lick hers up with noisy slurps. On came the newsreel, flashing black and white.

"When does the movie start?" asked Matilda, through a mouthful of snowy icecream. She wished the newsreel man would not speak so loudly.

"Shhh!" said Frances, embarrassed.

"WILL SHE STAY OR WILL SHE GO? THE QUESTION EVERYONE IN AUSTRALIA IS ASKING," shouted the newsreel man.

A face shot up on the screen, smiling, round, black and white. Matilda stared at it, startled. She swallowed a large mouthful of icecream in one go, and her throat tightened with cold.

That man, he looked just like her man, her tennis-ball

119

man, the man in the house next door! But how could a man next door be on a newsreel? She wanted to turn and say something to Elizabeth or Frances, but of course they didn't know about her man, only she knew.

Then the newsreel stopped and the man's face disappeared. The cartoons began and Matilda forgot all about the man, she was too busy laughing. Frances and Elizabeth both told her to be quiet again and again. "It's not even funny," Elizabeth said, but that made Matilda laugh even more. She couldn't help it. Once she had laughed so much at a cartoon that she swallowed a tooth. It was loose, hanging on a thread of pink gum, and down her throat it went. Then she cried because she wouldn't get a penny from the Tooth Fairy, but their mother rang the Tooth Fairy to explain what had happened, and there was a penny in the glass of water the next morning.

Finally it was time for *Roman Holiday*. Everybody in the theatre clapped and whistled.

"This is more news," said Matilda crossly. "When does the film start?"

"This is the film, silly," said Elizabeth. "It's just pretend news."

A lady in a long white dress and a tiny little crown was standing in the middle of a grand ballroom.

"That's the Queen!" said Matilda, excited.

"No it's not," said Elizabeth. "It's a story."

"It is so the Queen," retorted Matilda but Elizabeth kicked her in the ankle and told her to shut up.

It wasn't the Queen after all, it was a princess, who looked a bit like the photograph of their mother's friend Yvonne a thousand miles away, except Yvonne had sunglasses. This princess looked far away too, and when she smiled it was like someone from another country who couldn't understand English.

"How do you do," said the princess, "so glad you could come, I am delighted, you may sit down. You may sit down, so glad you could come."

The princess had to stand up for such a long, long time and her feet were sore and she kept taking them out of her shoes to rub them until one shoe fell off, but nobody could bend down and pick it up because she was a princess and it would be rude. Matilda wriggled in her seat.

"Is this going to be a long film?" she asked Elizabeth.

"Shhh," said Elizabeth.

After the party was over, the princess went to bed, but she was cross with her mother and had a nervous breakdown, just like Elizabeth. And a doctor came and gave her an injection with a big needle to make her get better, but it didn't work. So the princess crept out of the palace in the middle of the night, and fell asleep on the street till a man came along and found her.

How strange people sounded in films! Of course, they had American accents but it wasn't only that. They weren't like people to Matilda, they were like giant dolls. The air around her smelt of sugar and salt and was thick with whispering and the sound of kisses. On the screen the man and the princess were in a cave, and there was a face in the rock with an open mouth.

"If you put your hand in the mouth, and you are a liar, it will eat your hand up," someone in the film said.

The princess put her hand out, a little white hand, just like the Queen's but without a glove. She was shaking. She put it closer, closer – but then she pulled it back.

"I don't want to," the princess said.

She's afraid, thought Matilda.

"Go on!" shouted a boy sitting behind them.

"I can't!" said the princess. "I'm afraid!"

But the man in the film was not afraid. He put his hand up to the stone mouth. "If I am a liar, it will eat me," he said. He put his hand right inside it. Suddenly he fell forward, as though he was being pulled down into the dark cave. The princess screamed. So did Matilda.

"Shhh!" said Elizabeth and Frances together.

Matilda looked around the dark theatre. Across from where they were sitting was a statue of someone in a funny hat, hidden behind a gate, like a prison. Matilda didn't like it. She didn't like any of the statues. There were too many of them, everywhere you turned someone made of stone was looking at you with empty pale eyes. There were heads as well as whole bodies and they made her feel sick, like the taste of dark chocolate.

"I have to go to the toilet," she said to her sisters and she didn't wait for an answer, she got up and went by herself, up to the back of the theatre where there was a sign lit up: LADIES. Matilda slid up on the furry red-carpeted floor to the swinging door, and pushed it open with both hands.

Matilda stepped into the middle of the room, astonished. This Ladies was the most beautiful bathroom she had ever seen. It was like opening a door and walking into fairyland. All about her was gold and red and shiny and the walls were covered with painted butterflies, everywhere there were butterflies. There were even butterflies on the ceiling, and above the basin where you washed your hands there was a golden-edged mirror in the shape of a butterfly.

Then, to one side of the mirror, she saw a little sofa with red velvet cushions and curly golden legs. Matilda tossed off her sandals and lay down on the sofa in her socks.

"This is the life," she thought dreamily.

That was something people said in films. "This is the life." She could hear the dim sounds of the film now through the bathroom door. She didn't want to go back out there. She stood up and padded over to the basin with the beautiful golden taps, then up on her tiptoes she looked at herself inside the mirror, inside the butterfly wings, frosted and sparkling, spread flat.

"Hello," she said.

"Hello, Matilda," said Matilda in the mirror.

She shivered. Mirrors can't talk, she reminded herself, only in stories. Like little Karen's mirror in the fairytale, "You are more than pretty – you are beautiful." Then she remembered the little oblong mirror in the shiny black car from the house next door, and the driver looking at her and winking. But not really looking at her, because it was only the mirror.

"They're spies." That's what Floreal had said about the men next door. Maybe that was why the tennis-ball man was on the newsreel, thought Matilda suddenly. Spies could be in films, they weren't like real people.

Clapping and whistling and shouting came under the door. The film must have ended. Matilda spun around on her socked feet as the door of the bathroom swung open.

Fifteen

"MATILDA, THERE YOU ARE!" said Elizabeth, stepping inside the most beautiful bathroom in the world. She did not even seem to notice all the butterflies. "Come on, it's over. We're leaving."

A line of women were following after her. Matilda put her sandals back on and went with Elizabeth out to the theatre. The heavy red curtain had closed over the screen and the lights were coming on, like sunrise. There were so many people, crowding up the sloping aisles – where was Frances? When Matilda saw a space, she stopped and tried to stand on her hands, but it turned into a lopsided cartwheel.

"Hey, you, none of that!" came a voice from the wide, grand balcony above them. A man in a bow tie tapped sharply on the edge of the railing with his torch, clink. "Behave yourself."

There was Frances, waiting for them at the EXIT. Elizabeth seized a hand of each sister, and dragged them out through all the bodies into the glare of the open street.

"Where's Mummy?" asked Matilda, squinting to shield her eyes from the sudden daylight. She felt strange, as though while she was in the theatre she had forgotten that the world was still there, waiting for them outside.

There was a long queue of people for the next showing of the film, stretching up along the footpath. They couldn't see their mother and Uncle Paul anywhere.

"We'll just have to wait," said Elizabeth. "Let's go up here, out of the way."

She pointed across the road at a big department store. It was closed now, it was the afternoon.

"I'm hungry," said Matilda.

"Just sit here," said Elizabeth. "They won't be long."

There was a little wall, just big enough to sit on, in front of the shop window. Frances and Matilda squashed themselves onto it. Behind the glass were men's suits, bodies without heads and wigged heads without bodies with ties around their necks.

"Did you like the film?" asked Matilda.

"It was all right," said Frances.

"I loved it," said Elizabeth. She closed her eyes, smiling

to herself, as though she was thinking about it.

"I didn't like it," said Matilda.

They waited. None of them had a watch, but after all the people had gone inside the cinema, the city was almost silent. Sometimes a bus went past, or a car. Frances chewed on her fingernails. Matilda drew little figures in the dirt on the shop window with her finger. Every now and then she spat on the glass, rubbed her picture out and started again.

"Are you girls waiting for someone?" said a lady, stopping, but they looked away because they were not allowed to talk to strangers.

"Where's Mummy?" said Matilda. "I'm thirsty."

They heard the chimes from the Town Hall clock. Time was passing even though they couldn't see it.

"The Easter Bunny's coming tomorrow," said Matilda.

"Only if you're good," said Elizabeth.

"I am good," retorted Matilda. "I'm very good." She wished her mother and Uncle Paul would come.

A man walked over to them. "Where are your parents?" he demanded. They looked away.

At last they came, their mother and Uncle Paul. He was drunk. Their mother's face looked as though she had been crying.

"Three little maids in blue!" exclaimed Uncle Paul.

"Yellow," said Matilda, pointing at her daisy dress. She wrinkled her nose. "You smell awful," she said. "Like a man."

"And you are a grub," replied Uncle Paul, who liked

smelling like a man. "Look at you, black all over your face. What have you been doing, making mud pies?"

"These children belong to you?" said a man in a wide white hat. "You should be ashamed of yourselves. They've been sitting here over an hour."

"Piss off," said Uncle Paul.

"You should be ashamed," said the man.

"I am ashamed," replied Uncle Paul grandly. "I was born ashamed."

"Let's go," said their mother. "Let's go home."

"But I want to go to your hotel," Matilda reminded Uncle Paul. "You promised. We've been waiting hours."

"I'd like to get a drink," said Elizabeth.

"Me too," said Frances.

Uncle Paul shrugged at their mother.

"A drink it is," he said. "Just a quick one."

He swung Matilda up on his shoulders in one giant sweeping movement. Now she was the tallest person in the whole world. They walked away from the beautiful theatre, down towards the harbour, the flash of blue water and the grey, curling bridge.

All the shops were closed as they wandered past on the way to Uncle Paul's hotel. Behind the glass were Easter eggs, wrapped in wide ribbons.

"How was *Roman Holiday*?" asked Uncle Paul. "Did it make you cry?"

"It was boring," said Matilda. "It was so boring."

"It was all right," said Frances.

"I loved it," said Elizabeth.

Uncle Paul's hotel was on the corner of George Street, just up from Circular Quay. He slid Matilda down from his shoulders and put his arm around their mother's waist.

"Mind your manners, chickens," he murmured.

The girls followed Uncle Paul and their mother inside. It was wooden and dark. The carpet was green and it smelt stale. There was a man smoking and reading the paper. He looked up and nodded at Uncle Paul.

"Is this it?" said Matilda, unbelieving.

"This is it," said Uncle Paul.

The walls of the room were brick and there were paintings of cliffs and boats. Over in one corner there was a piano, covered with a blue cloth. There were chairs and round tables.

"Why aren't there any people?" asked Elizabeth, looking around.

"They only come alive at night," Uncle Paul said. "Like vampires."

"What's vampires?" asked Matilda.

"There's no such thing," said Frances.

Their mother looked so tired. She sat down in one of the chairs and laid her head down on the table in front of her, her perfect hair spreading like spilled flowers.

"Can we see your room?" said Matilda to Uncle Paul. "Where you sleep?"

"Against the rules, I'm afraid, pal," said Uncle Paul. "No visitors."

He went away, and came back with a big jug of lemonade and five glasses. The liquid spat like fire as he poured it out, one for each of them. They sipped their lemonade in silence through straws.

Uncle Paul took out a cigarette and lit it.

"Can you do smoke rings?" asked Matilda.

"Could if I wanted to," said Uncle Paul.

"Remember when we went to the Basin?" said Elizabeth abruptly. "And you showed us that game with the matches?"

Their mother's shoulders stiffened.

"I peeled that day," said Matilda, wanting to say something in a hurry. "It was so hot. I got sunburnt. I peeled all over. Peeled and peeled and peeled and peeled and peeled."

She remembered the long sheets of translucent skin that came off her face, her arms and legs. She had eaten some of them.

"I ate my own skin," said Matilda.

"That's disgusting," said Frances, finishing her lemonade. "You're a cannibal."

"Cannibals eat other people," Matilda corrected her. Even she knew that. "I only ate myself."

The man who had been reading the newspaper at the front desk came and sat down with them. Matilda didn't like him, she hoped he would go away soon. But Uncle Paul offered him a cigarette.

"Been to the Show yet, kids?" said the man, lighting up.

"Shhh!" Uncle Paul tapped the table. "Sore point."

"You poor little beggars," said the man and his eyes disappeared in crinkles.

He pushed the paper over to Uncle Paul.

"What do you think of all that?"

All what? Matilda wondered, looking down at the newsprint, all those rows of black letters. There was only one word that she could make out, a big R, a big E, and a big D—

"Ah, it's a cold, cold war," said Uncle Paul. He took a long draught of his cigarette and leaned back in his chair.

"What's a cold war?" asked Frances. Her straw was soggy now, and she pushed it about in her glass.

"It's when the whole world turns to ice," said Elizabeth in a dreamy voice.

"Isn't that the ice age, darling?" Uncle Paul blew smoke out from under his moustache. "Frozen dinosaurs and all that?"

The hotel was dirty, it felt sad. The chairs made creaking sounds and smelt of old clothes. Matilda didn't want to hear about wars. Weren't all the wars over, now that she was born?

"My snail hotel was better than this," she said grumpily, kicking her legs under her seat.

"Shhh, Matilda," said their mother.

"I told you, you wouldn't like it." Uncle Paul waved a finger at her. "I told you it's not for little girls."

The Sun Herald

HOLIDAY CROWDS IN BIG ROAD TANGLE

Sydney tied itself in knots yesterday getting to and from the holiday attractions.

The Royal Show, Doncaster meeting and Randwick race course, and Rugby League match-of-the-day at the Cricket Ground resulted in a record maze of traffic in the Moore Park area.

Between 4 p.m. and 5 p.m. more than 550 buses and trams, each making two trips, moved 100, 000 people from the Showground, Cricket Ground and Randwick races.

Red Suicide Squads In Heart Of French Fort

From Our Staff Correspondent And A.A.P.

NEW YORK, Saturday.— Suicide squads of Communist-led Vietminh rebels have cut still more trenches less than 800 yards from the heart of the French Indo-China outpost of Dienbienphu.

The French High Commission says it has halted the thrust, but expects a mass attack at any moment.

Sixteen

EASTER SUNDAY, 18 APRIL 1954

WHEN MATILDA OPENED HER EYES on Easter Sunday morning, she saw at once there was a chocolate Easter egg at the end of her bed!

She reached down, snatched up the egg, and bit the top off it. It cracked and she lay back and let the chocolate melt inside her mouth. Then she ate a bit more and a bit more and a bit more and then it was all gone. Matilda licked the chocolate off her teeth and skipped out into the kitchen. Uncle Paul was there, making tea.

"So, did the Easter Bunny come?" he inquired.

"Yes," said Matilda. "I got a chocolate egg!"

"What do you know?" Uncle Paul was shocked. "And I got nuffin'."

Matilda sat down at the kitchen table, watching Uncle Paul pour two cups of tea, out the spout of the blue and white teapot through the silver strainer. He left the room, a teacup in each hand.

"He shouldn't be here when your father is away," said Floreal. "I told you before."

"What would you know?" Matilda poked out her tongue. "Anyway, Daddy's coming home soon."

Leave me alone, she thought. Go back into the radio and leave me alone.

Outside, the sky was grey, and the air felt damp as though it might rain. Matilda was thirsty after all that chocolate. She knelt down next to the garden tap under the tree growing under her bedroom window with the bright red berries, to get a drink from the hose. Matilda liked the water from the hose, it was cool and tasted of earth and metal. You weren't allowed to water the garden because of the drought, but at least you were still allowed to drink.

As she gulped down mouthfuls of dripping water, she noticed the mad old man from the house next door standing on his pathway, gesturing at her.

Does he want me to come in? Matilda didn't want to at all, not after last time. She pretended not to see. But then she heard his slow footsteps coming towards her, shuffling along, and the stick clicking.

"Ha!" said the mad old man, when he was near enough.

"Hallo," replied Matilda reluctantly.

"Where'd you all go, yesterday?"

He said "yesterday" a funny way, it sounded like "yesterdee".

"To town, to the pictures," answered Matilda, turning off the hose.

"Ha!"

The mad old man came a little closer. He smelt of wet wool. He looked as though he was about to say something else, when the noise of a car skidding too fast down their steep street stopped him. They both turned and saw the sleek black car, braking noisily outside the yellow house. Two men in suits and hats got out and went straight inside.

The old man turned back to Matilda. "You know them, eh?"

"No," said Matilda. They were different men, they weren't the ones she knew.

"I've seen you," said the old man unpleasantly. "I've seen you watching them."

Matilda was annoyed. He must have been watching her watching them, if that was the case.

"I'm just being a spy," she said. "They're spies, so I'm just spying back."

"Spies?" repeated the mad old man. "What do you mean, spies?"

He was very close to her now and his eyes were black and sharp, like a lizard's.

"What do you mean, spies?" and his peeling fingers clutched the top of his walking stick. "You shouldn't say things like that."

"I saw that man on the newsreel," said Matilda crossly, but she stepped back, not wanting to be so near. "So they are so spies!"

The mad old man said nothing then. Matilda wondered if he had even heard her. But he stood staring hard at the big pale house, as she shook her wet hands up and down in the air, scattering tiny drops all over the dry land.

Seventeen

EASTER SUNDAY, 18 APRIL 1954

ON SUNDAY AFTERNOON IT RAINED, at last it rained. Elizabeth went out for a walk, and got soaking wet. Frances lay in bed, reading and eating her chocolate egg, sliver by sliver, so that it lasted all afternoon.

Their mother went to sleep.

"Is she sick?" asked Matilda, but Uncle Paul put a finger to his mouth.

"She'll be all right," he said. "She's just worried about your dad."

On the table in the kitchen was some of her mother's knitting. Matilda felt the wool between her fingers. It was a grey, bumpy jumper and it was for her, their mother said. It was taking such a long time to do, though, she was afraid that it would be too small by the time it was finished. You grow too fast, Mattie, their mother said. Nothing fits you any more.

Like Alice in Wonderland, thought Matilda. Only I will never be able to be small again. She could feel something sad underneath her somewhere, shifting like a little crab buried in sand.

"You grow too fast," her mother had said to Matilda in her swimsuit, the day they went to the Basin. "Nothing fits you any more."

"Bigger things fit me," Matilda had said.

They were at the barbecue ground of the Basin. Her mother was sitting on their picnic blanket in the sun. They had got off the ferry and wandered up with their things to the flat grassed area away from the beach. Their father was making a fire to cook the sausages. Matilda and Frances scuttled about in the bush, bringing him back twigs. He piled them up with dry leaves in the shape of a wigwam.

"Stand back, girls," he told them as he bent to light it.

The flames caught in moments and smoke rose up into the sky in a stream.

"A fine blaze," said Uncle Paul approvingly.

"Why don't you run off, all of you," said their father, "and have a swim before lunch. I'll call you when it's ready."

Their mother was opening the picnic basket, to find the meat. She looked up, and said in a sharp, anxious sort of voice, "Are you sure?"

"Please," said their father, and he bent down and took her hand and kissed it, like a prince in a story.

Then he did a strange thing. He put his arms around Uncle Paul and hugged him. He didn't look at anyone else.

So they left him. They took off their shoes and put them in a pile, even her mother's beautiful red shoes with the golden buckles. They picked up their towels and scrambled down the slippery rocks, Uncle Paul and their mother and the three girls, to the little curved beach to swim.

Frances and their mother dived straight in the water, swimming in circles around each other like dolphins. Matilda didn't feel like going in. She sat barefoot on a rock near the water's edge. She could feel her body burning, her skin was turning pink in front of her. We are white men in a black man's country, her teacher said on hot days when she shooed them into the shade of the weather shed and they all laughed because, of course, their teacher was not a man and neither were they.

Uncle Paul, hairy like a mammoth, sat on the beach with Elizabeth. He stood burnt matches, head up, in the damp sand.

"This is my army," he told Elizabeth. "You set up yours, come on. Anywhere you like."

Elizabeth set up her soldiers neatly in rows. This was before she had her nervous breakdown, when she used to do what people asked. The burnt ends of the matches looked like little black helmets. Matilda remembered how she had asked her father once whether the dead soldiers would still be in their uniforms when they were in heaven, with helmets and guns over their shoulders, like the statue in town for all the dead soldiers. But he said nobody wore clothes in heaven, they didn't need them any more. In heaven nobody needs anything at all, her father said.

Matilda liked the sound of that. She didn't much like clothes and shoes and ribbons. She liked arms and legs and teeth and fingernails. She liked her feet, and her toes. She liked the feeling of the wet sand under her feet, as she sat banging the waves with a long, light, dry-leaved branch.

"Five pebbles each," said Uncle Paul. "We take it in turns and see how many we can hit. You know, like the rifle range."

After a while, Frances and their mother came out of the water, shivering, wrapping themselves in towels.

"The meat must be cooked by now," said their mother. "Let's go up."

So they climbed up the sandy rocks back to the barbecue, but their father wasn't there.

"Where's Daddy?" said Elizabeth.

The food was all laid out on their blanket on the ground, warm meat and bread and tomato sauce and bottles of beer and lemonade. But their father wasn't there. Their mother looked white, even her lips were white.

"He must have gone for a walk," said Uncle Paul. "He'll be back."

"I'm hungry," said Matilda. "Can we eat?"

They sat on the blanket and ate and their mother brought out a packet of biscuits and a thermos of tea and still their father hadn't come back.

"What's he doing?" said their mother and Uncle Paul answered softly, "Just let him have a bit of time." Just a bit of time.

Elizabeth took a biscuit and walked over to the edge of the grass, looking out to the land where they lived far away. She kept walking, along the edge of the picnic ground, dragging a stick from the fire in the dirt behind her. Frances, restless, wandered away up to where other children were playing French cricket. She waited around at the edges of the game for a while until the ball came dribbling in her direction, and she picked it up and was part of it.

Then their mother said she was going to lie down in the shade and Uncle Paul said, Yes, good idea, I think I'll stretch my legs a bit.

So they all went away and Matilda was left alone on the blanket. She lay on her side for a moment, full of food. Right next to the blanket were her mother's red shoes that she had taken off before their swim. They glinted in the sunshine, red and gold and black.

Matilda reached out and picked one up. She looked around to see where her mother was, but she was flat on her back with a towel over her face, under the shade of a tree. Matilda kicked off her sandals. One at a time, she put her feet inside the red shoes. They were so small, she had to push her toes right down into them. Would she have feet as big as her mother's one day? It was hard to believe.

Matilda stood up in her mother's shoes. How tall she was! She took a tottering step forward. She had to be very careful to keep her balance so she held out her arms, like a tightrope walker.

"I'm the Queen," she said to herself, "the Queen on a picnic."

She forgot all about the giant sandcastle she had planned on making. This was much better. She could pretend she was the Queen on a boring picnic, who decided she would climb a tall tree to get away from all the bother of being a queen and having to shake people's hands and wave at the crowds. Sometimes the Queen must feel like climbing a tree, thought Matilda, everybody did.

She staggered off in the red shoes in the direction of the bush, away from the picnic area. She nearly fell over, but the ground was soft and sandy and she managed to keep upright by bending her knees. She was heading for the very tallest tree. That's what the Queen would do, Matilda reasoned, queens like the biggest of everything.

It wasn't easy getting up into the first branch, and her feet were slippery with sweat inside the shoes. But then she pulled as hard as she could and the branches stretched up like a ladder into the sky and it seemed she could go on climbing for ever.

When she leaned back to catch her breath, she looked down at the world underneath her and was amazed by how high she had climbed. She could see the whole picnic ground. The children and the grown-ups, the old people on stools playing cards, and the cliffs and the grey and white water and a ferry leaving and further out yachts with white sails. She could even see as far as the half-hidden houses where rich people lived who only came to the mainland on their little motorboats with big dogs to buy fruit and meat.

If I lived there I would not come out for anything, thought Matilda. *I would eat snakes like the Aborigines.* Matilda had never in her life seen an Aborigine, but in the school library there was a book of photographs of children with the whitest teeth, laughing, leaping into water. Her father told her that Aborigines used to live in the bush around where their house was. *That must have been before the cowboys and Red Indians came*, decided Matilda.

But now she was safe from guns and bows and arrows, up high in the tallest tree in the Basin, with its white peeling trunk and leaves smelling of cough drops. *I can see everything*, Matilda thought, *I can see the whole Basin.* She could see everything, silver and grey like mirrors, like moths, she saw everything, high in the tallest tree.

But as she was looking, she saw something down in the bush and she didn't understand. She wanted to look away, but she couldn't. She kept looking, and she was afraid.

She was so afraid she jerked and started to slide down the warm trunk and she nearly fell off, right off the tree down onto the ground way below. But then she remembered Yvonne's little brother and his lost brains, and just in time she grabbed a branch above her and saved herself.

She saved herself, but her foot slipped underneath her. And down from the tree, down from her right foot into the depths of the grey-green bush, fell her mother's red shoe.

The Sydney Morning Herald

Dry Spell Ends In Sydney

Sydney yesterday had its highest rainfall for seven weeks.

Fifty-one points of rain fell in the measured period 9 a.m. to 9 p.m., most of it in a shower soon after 4 p.m.

PARTY AT EMBASSY

EASTER SIGHTSEERS made the Embassy a point of call and many sat in parked cars watching for signs of activity among the Russians.

Last night there was an Easter party at the Embassy attended only by Embassy staff. It was probably also a farewell to Mrs. Petrov.

Telephone callers to the Embassy heard lively women's voices and laughter in the background.

Lights outside the building blazed throughout the night, and inside the Embassy lights showed behind the blinds in almost every room.

The Sydney Morning Herald

FEAR OF DEATH

Nothing was so detrimental to health as fear, the Rev. Gordon Powell said at St. Stephen's Presbyterian Church yesterday.

He said: "Chronic fear can produce all kinds of physical complaints from headaches to dermatitis and paralysis.

"The greatest fear of all is the fear of death, and in one form or other this fear lies at the back of almost every other fear ... Irresponsible talk about the hydrogen bomb can produce abnormal and epidemic fear to the great hurt of the people.

"Jesus Christ had no more fear of death than he had of sleeping."

TEST FOR POLIO

Yellow Tinge To Skin

ADELAIDE, Saturday.— An Adelaide doctor has made an important medical discovery that polio causes a yellowish skin tinge ... He has found the tinge most noticeable around the nose and on the palms and soles ... The test merely involves examination of a patient's palms under filtered ultra-violet light.

If the patient is suffering from polio or certain other virus brain infections the palms appear yellowish-green instead of the normal dusky blue under such light.

Eighteen

EASTER MONDAY, 19 APRIL 1954

ON MONDAY THERE WAS STILL no school because it was a public holiday. Their mother sat by the phone, dialling number after number again, to see if she could find their father. Matilda lay on her stomach in the living room, listening to her, cutting paper into little pieces. It took her a long time because she was left-handed and the scissors would not go the way she wanted.

It was hard being left-handed. At school when they did writing, she always made a mess of the letters on the page. The teacher hit her on the hand with a feather duster.

"You don't even try," the teacher said.

Perhaps her teacher was right, Matilda thought sadly, perhaps she didn't try. She thought she did, but perhaps she didn't really. Just as she thought she believed in God but didn't really, not like Catholics.

"Can we go to the Show today?" asked Matilda.

"No," said their mother.

"Why not?"

"We can't, Elizabeth's sick in bed," said her mother, because Elizabeth had caught a cold from her walk in the rain the day before.

"We can leave her behind," said Matilda.

She tossed up all the little bits of white paper she'd been cutting into the air, so they floated about her like tiny little snowflakes.

"Will Daddy come home soon?" asked Matilda.

No answer.

"When's Daddy coming home, anyway?" said Matilda.

"I don't know." Her mother stood in the middle of the room, her hands in her hair. "I just don't know."

"Come here." Uncle Paul beckoned to Matilda from the piano. "I want to show you something."

Matilda went over. Uncle Paul lifted her in the air in his big hands and stood her on the stool. Then he opened the top lid of the piano.

"It's like seeing inside a person," he murmured, "like cutting them open and seeing what's there."

Matilda gazed inside. How full it was! There was a long, curved row of hammers, one for every key, Uncle Paul was saying, and then a line of hard strings like a harp. When you pressed a key, a hammer shot forward and hit one of the strings. That's what made the sound of the note.

Ping! Ping! Pang!

"Hey presto!" cried Uncle Paul. "All mysteries revealed."

Keys were made from elephant tusks, Uncle Paul said. Funny, wasn't it? So many dead elephants just for piano keys.

"You know what he did, don't you?" said Floreal, right in Matilda's ear.

The lid of the piano slid from Uncle Paul's fingers and closed with a sharp bang like a gunshot. Matilda jolted, she nearly tumbled from the stool. Uncle Paul grabbed her just in time.

In the bathroom, Matilda crushed up some toilet paper and put it in her ears, so she wouldn't hear Floreal any more. Then she went out to the laundry to watch their mother wash the clothes. The laundry was hot and the clothes were so heavy, but how strong their mother was! She didn't look strong but she was underneath. She was like a rainbow ball that you couldn't crack with your teeth, the only way to eat it up was to suck it until all at once it was gone, you couldn't even say when.

When the washing was over, Matilda followed her out the back to help her hang the clothes to dry. She held the pieces of clothing up one by one while her mother pegged. The wind blew the clothesline around and around like a merry-go-round.

There was a lot of talking noise from the garden next door. Matilda felt nervous. What if one of the men came over to the fence and spoke to her? Then their mother might find out about the lift in the black car, and how angry she would be.

"That's done, then," said their mother.

Her voice sounded strange because she had a wooden peg in her mouth. Matilda looked at her anxiously. They went back inside the house.

"What are you going to do now?"

Her mother didn't answer. She picked up a knife next to the sink, and began peeling potatoes and letting them drop into a bowl of water. Then she started to cry and Uncle Paul came over. He took the knife from her hand and laid it down on the bench.

"Where is he?" she said, wiping her face. "Where can he be?"

"Don't get in a state," said Uncle Paul, putting his arm around her.

Matilda put her finger in the bowl and pushed the peeled potatoes around. They looked like giant pale pebbles. Then she ran out of the kitchen, down to her room. Frances was lying on the bed, reading. Matilda sat cross-legged on the carpet.

"I hate Uncle Paul," she said out loud.

Frances looked over briefly, but she kept on reading. The carpet was dusty, it made Matilda's nose itch and she sneezed. Then she remembered the giant lollipop, her wonderful prize, rotting in the darkness under the bed where she had left it. She lifted up the hanging bedclothes and reached out until her fingers found the wooden handle.

She sat up and inspected her prize. Some of the cellophane had rolled away and sugar had seeped through. Little bits of green wool from the carpet were stuck to it, like a green beard on a round face.

"Maybe if I gave it to Mummy," thought Matilda suddenly, "that might make her feel better."

She glanced over at Frances, but she was still reading. Matilda quickly left the room with her prize and went down the hall to her parents' bedroom.

The door was half open. Matilda pushed on it gently, and peeped around.

Her mother was sitting on the bed, alone, with her head bent, and she was holding one red shoe in her lap, sobbing softly to herself. The lollipop slipped out of Matilda's hands silently and fell on the floor.

Nineteen

UP IN THE HIGHEST TREE IN THE BASIN, *the red shoe had tumbled down down from Matilda's foot, down into the tangled bush.*

Matilda clung to the warm trunk and heard the cicadas and bird calls in the wind and the lapping of the water on the world. She smelt the gum leaves and just next to her nose was a streak of sticky sap, glinting like the trail left behind by a snail. Her heart was beating hard.

Someone shouted and then someone else, but not about the shoe. Matilda looked down and saw her mother running through the bush and crying out, screaming, "Help me, help me! Someone help me!"

Matilda must have climbed down then, though she didn't remember doing it, but she must have because there she was and she could feel the vibrations of people running past her up through the ground and eyes were staring at her and there were flies everywhere. She didn't know where anyone was, not Frances or Elizabeth, but she could hear her mother crying somewhere far away.

Then a man she didn't know grasped hold of her and wouldn't let her go. He told her to sit still, sit down, sit still, stay here love, they'll be all right. Matilda hid herself at the back of the trees and waited for someone to come.

She waited and waited and no one came. She took off the red shoe, and hugged it to her chest. She watched as people were packing up their picnic things, ready for the last ferry back to Palm Beach. Would nobody come? It was twilight and the ocean was silver in the sunset.

"Matilda, there you are!" said Uncle Paul, coming forward in the half-dark.

"Where's Mummy?" asked Matilda, frightened.

"Down at the wharf," replied Uncle Paul.

She couldn't see his face properly, just a blur and the smell of him. He was smoking.

"I'm sorry," Matilda whispered, "I lost one of Mummy's shoes," and she held the remaining shoe up to him.

Uncle Paul took it. He didn't seem to understand.

"Your dad had a bit of an accident," he said, stubbing out his cigarette. "Come on, let's get on the boat."

Over at the wharf, people were huddled together as the ferry came in, like refugees escaping from the war that Matilda had seen in newsreels. There was Elizabeth and Frances, and their father and their mother. There they all were, safe and sound.

No one spoke. Uncle Paul gave their mother the red shoe, but she put it on absent-mindedly, leaving her other foot bare. She was gripping their father's arm, but he stared out at the moon on the water, as though he was alone.

Matilda held Elizabeth's hand as the ferry approached, gliding towards them like a floating palace, its windows glowing. It creaked and banged against the pillars of the jetty, and the wood made cracking sounds. Up flew the thick brown rope, catching the hook of the wharf like a lasso. The deckhand thrust the gangplank across the black water between the boat and the land. All the picnickers picked up their bags and baskets and moved murmuring forward across the little bridge into the warmth of the boat.

Elizabeth, Frances and Matilda sat with their father and mother and Uncle Paul, inside the cabin, next to the engine where the metal wall was hot. Their father slumped forward, his eyes closed. Their mother had her head in her hands. Matilda could hear her moaning faintly, Help me, help me.

Uncle Paul tapped Matilda on the shoulder. She was bright red on every part of her skin that you could see.

"You're going to peel like a potato tomorrow," he said.

It was too hot in there and it smelt of machines.

Matilda slid off the seat and went out to the cool open deck. The benches were full of people and hats and towels and baskets and sand, sweat and seawater. The only place for her was the wooden life raft. She climbed up onto it and lay down on her back.

Then a voice somewhere underneath her, floating upwards like a balloon, said, "That poor woman."

"It's the war that does it to them," said a second voice.

"He'll try it again, you know," said a third voice.

The boat rocked as it pushed forward through the waves, and the moon was a perfect half and yellow as teeth.

"Three little kids."

"Remember that fellow at the club."

"Lucky they got there in time."

"Too sad."

"He looked all right."

"You can't tell."

"Lucky they saw him."

"Lucky for who?"

"You never know what's waiting for you round the corner, do you?"

"What a place to do it."

"In the middle of the bush."

"At Christmas time."

"He brought the rope with him, you know, in the picnic basket."

"He planned it all."

"Those poor little children."

"What a world."

"What next?"

"Poor woman, poor woman."

"How will she cope?"

Poor woman, poor woman. All those poor people, thought Matilda, remembering the news that morning, and how her mother had been so upset, those poor people who fell out of the train, down to the bottom of the river in New Zealand, those poor little dead children. All those poor sailors dead in the war lying at the bottom of the ocean, ping, ping, ping, all those poor people far away where bombs fell, with no homes left and all their children dead like a ladybird.

Poor woman. Poor woman, poor little children. All disappeared from the face of the earth. The engine of the ferry changed gear, and the boat was slowing down. They were coming into Palm Beach. Matilda felt the motor chugging underneath her through her bones, like blood through her heart.

The Sydney Morning Herald

OFFICIALS DRAG MRS. PETROV INTO AIRCRAFT

"Help Me" Appeal To Crowd Reported

ONE THOUSAND struggling, fighting and screaming people at Kingsford Smith Airport last night attempted to stop Mrs. Evdokia Petrov from returning to Russian…

WILD RUSH AS CAR ARRIVES

Mrs. Petrov was dressed in a grey suit and blue hat on arrival at the airport but her clothing was crushed, crumpled and disarranged, and she had lost a shoe before she finally boarded the plane.

Police found it impossible to keep back the crowds of New Australians, who began shouting "Don't let her go."

Within a few seconds the whole crowd at the airport had taken up the chant.

As Mrs. Petrov walked towards the aircraft, tension mounted in the crowd.

When she was being photographed, Mrs. Petrov tried to smile, but she broke down, covered her face with both hands and appeared to sag at the knees.

The Russian couriers on both sides of her then half-dragged and half-carried her around the back of the plane to the gangway.

Statutory declarations were made by some of the people at the airport after the plane had left. They claimed that they heard Mrs. Petrov say she wanted to stay.

One of these, signed Konstantyn Salwarosky, of 33 Pitt Street, Waterloo, read: "Tonight as Mme. Petrov was leaving Mascot, I saw her coming round the back way on to the entrance into the plane.

"She was struggling against the Russians trying to push her in.

"I heard her say in Russian: "Ja nie chat chu. (I do not want to go)."

> Tuesday, APRIL 20, 1954 <

Last Day Of Show To-day

◄○►

To-day, the last day of the Royal Show, will be children's day, with a programme especially designed for youngsters.

Twenty

EASTER TUESDAY, 20 APRIL 1954

TUESDAY WAS STILL A HOLIDAY from school and their father still hadn't come home. Frances was in her room, thinking. She had decided that she wanted to grow up very soon. She didn't like being a child any more and she didn't like living in their house. She used to, but not now. It was all different, she didn't know why.

She laid her warm cheek against the cool pane of glass of the window. When had it happened, that she had stopped liking it? She thought it might have been round the time Elizabeth had her nervous breakdown, but perhaps it was before that.

Whenever it was, she knew she wanted to be grown-up and live in her own house. She wanted to be twenty-one. That's what a grown-up was. When I am twenty-one, Mark and I will have been married for five years, thought Frances, remembering what Mark had said. We will have our own babies then, and I will wear an apron and every Friday Mark will bring me a box of Old Gold chocolates.

But Mark had disappeared. They said he had polio.

"No," said Frances, shaking her head.

She didn't believe it. Perhaps she could go and find him, find where he lived, discover what really happened. Why hadn't she thought of it before? Mark's house was not far from their school. His mother used to come to the playground every afternoon to pick him up. Everyone knew Mark's mother. Mark's mother was enormous, she wore great big dresses without sleeves and her back was broad and covered all over with flies, hundreds of them. The children laughed at Mark and pointed because his mother was fat, but Mark didn't mind. He walked to where she waited for him, every afternoon, and took her hand.

One day Frances had followed them, without really meaning to. She'd been watching as they left the playground, and seen Mark pick some purple flowers that grew wild on the side of the street and give them to his mother. Then they'd gone on down the road, round a corner and up another street to their house, inside a gate, down a path, inside a door. Frances had stood with her scooter at a distance, watching. She remembered that the front fence was decorated with little coloured tiles. It was not like the fences of the other houses. It was beautiful, like a mosaic in a church.

I'll know it when I see it, thought Frances. A kind of excitement was creeping over her. She could find him! She could go today! She could ride on her scooter to his house and go in the gate and up the path and knock on his door and say, Mark, Mark, where have you been? Where did you go? I'm here, it's me, Frances. Remember? I've been waiting for you, we are going to be married.

In a moment she had got herself out of bed and dressed in her shorts and sandals.

"I'm going out on my scooter for a while," she announced as she walked into the kitchen. "I don't want any breakfast." She didn't want to wait, not for a second.

Uncle Paul smacked himself on the forehead in shock.

"She speaks!" he cried.

"By yourself?" asked Matilda.

"Yes," replied Frances determinedly.

"What a good idea," said their mother, trying to smile, but her eyes were somewhere else. "Let me pack you something to eat."

She cut Frances a vegemite sandwich and wrapped it up in greaseproof paper, and gave her a little bottle of water.

"Where do you think you'll go?" she asked, kissing her goodbye.

"I don't know," lied Frances.

She went quickly outside and put the sandwich and the drink bottle in the white wire basket of her scooter. She pumped up the tyres as high as she could, so she could fly on the air. Her father had told her that, when you ride on tyres you are riding on the air.

Frances had a strange feeling as she pushed on her scooter and began to slide away from her home, as though she was running away. No, not exactly that, it was more as though her home might not be there when she returned, that it would have disappeared into mist like a vanishing palace in a fairytale.

One of the black cars from the big house came down the hill past her, then another one, then another one. They're driving too fast, thought Frances, they might kill someone. She pushed harder on the road, to get away as quickly as she could.

By the time she reached the top of the hill where the school was, she was already sweating and her head itched. She stopped and took a sip of water out of the drink bottle. The playground on the other side of the school gate was empty, of course, empty concrete and grass, empty trees, empty monkey bars and swings, like a haunted house.

Maybe it was haunted – there were stories about things that had happened at the school in the olden days. A boy who had fallen out of a window, a teacher who died of a heart attack during a thunderstorm. When Frances was in second class, there had been a big storm full of thunder and lightning and their teacher had made them all get under their desks until it was over, as though bombs were

161

dropping from little aeroplanes in the sky. Their teacher had clutched her grey bun and sunk under her own desk at the front of the classroom, waving her ruler in the air. It was a big thick ruler with pictures of boomerangs on it.

Frances started on her scooter again. This was where she had to think. She had to try to remember the direction that Mark and his mother had walked. She glided past the houses, the trees, past hard yellow front lawns and thorny rose bushes and children running, past neat white fences and broken rusting fences and letterboxes. She could hear a baby crying from somewhere inside as she went past, crying and crying.

Matilda had cried like that when she was a baby, wrapped up in a sheet. Frances had been four when Matilda was born. A lady down the road had come and cooked their dinner while their mother was in hospital. She had made rice pudding. Frances didn't like it at all, she had pretended to eat it and then spat it out in the back yard.

How Matilda had cried when she came home! When their mother unwrapped her, Matilda's little red toes stood apart and shook with rage as she cried.

"She's all right, really," said their mother. "All poor little babies cry."

"Why?" asked Frances.

"Because they can't talk," said their mother.

Frances knew she must be getting close to Mark's house and she started to feel anxious. She wanted to see Mark, but what if he really did have polio? What if he was one

162

of those children she had seen in the newsreel, that had to lie in bed with an iron lung, that couldn't even breathe by themselves? Just lie in his room like little Karen in the fairy story she had read to Matilda, little Karen with her wooden feet who could never go to church with all the other children but just looked sadly at her crutches and cried out, "O God! Help me!"

And suddenly she was there. She knew even before she saw the stony fence, because there was Mark's mother, unmistakable in the broad flowered dress, standing with a hose in her hand in the front yard of their house. Frances was transfixed by the stream of water coming out from the hose. What would she say? Now she was here, what would she say?

"Hallo," said Frances, stepping off her scooter while the wheels still spun.

Mark's mother turned around. Her hair was black and she had Mark's beautiful dark eyes. A little brown dog stood up from under the edge of the house and ambled over, wagging its ragged tail.

"Hallo," said Frances again.

"Hallo," said Mark's mother uncertainly.

"Um," said Frances, tightening her grip on the handle-bars. "Is Mark home?"

Mark's mother held out her hand towards Frances, the hand that was not holding the hose. She was shaking.

"You want to see Mark?" she said.

She had a funny voice. Was she foreign? Frances did not

know any foreign people. She did not know anybody who was not like her.

"Is he allowed to play?" she asked.

The water dribbled from the hose. The dog licked it up.

"They don't tell you?" said Mark's mother.

"Tell me what?" said Frances, feeling herself go still.

"Mark is dead," said Mark's mother. "Mark is dead."

Mark with his head down on his desk in the classroom, with the sunlight shining on his hair, always with his grey jumper on, even on the hottest days.

Mark's mother leaned back on the wall of the house. The hose fell on the ground. Then down fell the tears, large and terrifying.

"God help me," said Mark's mother.

But we are getting married, Frances wanted to say. We are getting married. He's inside, look for him, he's there. He's lying down inside in his room, waiting for me to come. He can't walk, but I can.

"He is in the cemetery," said Mark's mother, wiping her eyes, but more flowed out, on and on.

Mark wasn't dead, thought Frances, he couldn't be. He must be lying in his bed, waiting for her. In her mind she saw his black hair, his pink lips and his sleepy eyes, but she couldn't put them all together. It was like trying to imagine what someone you'd never seen looked like, someone who was dead before you were born.

If she went inside the house, surely he would be there! He would raise his head and smile at her, his slow, gentle smile, as though he had just woken up from a deep sleep, his lips red like her mother's red earrings, tiny drops of blood.

"You can see him, in the cemetery. You come with me, I take you," said Mark's mother, reaching out both hands to Frances.

I have to go away, thought Frances. I have to leave. I can't stay here.

She found some breath, gulped it in out of the blue sky around her.

"I have to go now," she said.

Her hair swept back in knots in the wind as she sped away, faster and faster. Her heart ached, her legs ached and she had a stitch. The smell and sound of the ocean was so very strong it was as though the waves were rolling inside her head from one ear to the other. There was a rumbling crack in the air, like thunder.

She left the street and all the houses, she flew away, past the school, the milkbar and the newsagent's.

HELP ME said big black letters on the newspaper posters outside. There was a rumbling crack in the air, like thunder. HELP ME said the newspaper poster, said Mark's mother. HELP ME, cried their mother that day at the Basin, God help me, cried little Karen. Help me, thought Frances.

"And her soul flew on the sunbeams to Heaven, and no one was there who asked after the Red Shoes."

Frances pushed with her foot then lifted it off the ground and began to skim downwards, bits of loose gravel spitting up on either side of her.

Twenty-one

EASTER TUESDAY, 20 APRIL 1954

IN ELIZABETH'S ROOM there was a crack in the curtain that let in just enough daylight to see the newsprint.

"*Ja nie chat chu,*" Elizabeth read out loud, sounding the words, curiously. "*Ja nie chat chu.* I do not want to go."

She was still in bed because of her cold. She didn't feel well, but she was tired of being inside. She had read all the papers, and now she was reading them over again.

"Mrs Petrov this morning visited, probably for the last time, the pleasant brick home she shared for three years with her husband. At the end of the visit, a bodyguard of three burly Russians pushed her into a black limousine."

Elizabeth felt sorry for Mrs Petrov, squashed in the back seat of the black limousine with three burly Russians. It would be hard to breathe, especially if they didn't let her open the window. Perhaps they would open it a tiny bit and she could put her nose out, like a dog. It would take hours to drive from Canberra to Sydney, and there would be nothing but dust and gum trees and cows. And it would be night. Mrs Petrov would look out and see nothing at all, as though she was at the ends of the earth.

Maybe they wouldn't let her even look out. Lenin was not allowed to look out when he took his secret train from Germany back to Russia to make the Revolution. Elizabeth had read about it in a history book in the school library. Black curtains had covered all the windows of the train carriage, so no one could see in or out. In the book there was a map of Europe, with a thick black dashed line that showed the route of his journey from west to east. Lenin wrapped up in black, making his way across Europe, all the way to beautiful, golden, cold, cold Russia, secretly and silently, like a fox.

Elizabeth folded the newspaper up. She couldn't read any more. She wanted to speak to her father, to explain to him why she couldn't go back to school. If she could just talk to him, then he would understand. But no one knew where he was, that was the problem. He should have come home by now. He was missing. Elizabeth knew this, although no one had told her. But she had listened to her mother and Uncle Paul, whispering, and all those desperate phone calls. Have you heard from him? Have you seen him? Where is he? Nobody knew where he was.

Perhaps he's still on his ship, thought Elizabeth. He's hiding in his cabin. Perhaps he's tired or frightened or perhaps he just forgot to get off. If he was on his ship, she could go to the post office and send him a telegram. A telegram could reach a ship.

Elizabeth had no money for a telegram. But she could steal some. She could go into a shop and take some out of the till when the shopkeeper wasn't looking. Or she could steal someone's purse.

"Whoever steals my purse steals nothing, it is trash."

That was Shakespeare – or was it? Trash was an American word, that's what they called garbage, so it couldn't be Shakespeare then. Words hummed in circles through her head. She was sick of them. She didn't want to think any more in words.

"True love need not necessarily end in death," said Elizabeth out loud, surprising herself.

What was that? Was it a poem? They had been reading a poem in class the day she'd had her nervous breakdown and came home with her plaits tied on top of her head. She remembered looking down at the page and seeing each word separately. The words do not want to be in this poem, she had realized. They want to stay apart from each other. It is not right that they should be all here in a row, made to mean something they don't want to mean. Then she had gone home on the bus and had her nervous breakdown.

Perhaps one day she would find a world where there were no more words. Elizabeth looked over at the paperweight that her father had given her, catching sunlight on the bookshelf, the little fish trapped in glass, its gold fins like floating leaves. Even with the curtains drawn, the glass gleamed and she could see the shadow of the fish. Under the sea it would be very dark and quiet, the sun wouldn't reach down there.

Under the sea it was always night, there was no counting of hours or minutes, there were no beginnings or endings of things to have to change clothes for, to eat meals by. Nobody spoke, there was no English or French or Russian, just bubbles rising up to the surface and disappearing, like shadows of submarines.

I would be safe down there, thought Elizabeth. Even the H-Bomb would not find me.

But it would be cold in the ocean, cold as Russia. Russia was full of snow, people froze to death in it. But Russia was beautiful, so much more beautiful than Australia. There was nothing beautiful in Australia, thought Elizabeth impatiently, it was all bush and ocean and tin roofs. In Russia the cities were built of shining, onion-shaped golden domes and deep, glorious music rose up out of them, like magic clouds. And people dressed in bear furs, and there were wet, lovely dark green forests filled with wolves.

Russia was beautiful, but in the small inky print that came off on Elizabeth's fingers, she read that in Russia there were Communists and that they were building a big bomb and planes would fly over and drop it and all the world would disintegrate in seconds, all the cities and roads and farms and people, all gone like a dream. Then there would be no more days and no more dreams.

Ja nie chat chu. I do not want to go.

She stood up from the bed and went over to the wardrobe she had hidden in the day her English teacher had come to visit. She took out her sandshoes, put them on and did up the laces in careful bows, twice over. She would go for a walk to the beach. She needed to walk. There would be nothing to think about except her feet rising from the earth and coming down again, her arms swinging and the world moving back and forth.

Elizabeth walked out of the quiet house, up the gravelled road, along the sandy pathways through the bush. By the time she reached the beach, a wind had risen and sand was scattering across the shore like a low fog.

She gazed out over the ocean. Her father was out there somewhere, standing on the deck of a ship with a telescope, wondering what he would find next. Like Jason, she thought, on board the *Argo* with his Argonauts, searching for the Golden Fleece. On Boxing Day, she had stood on the opposite shore at the Basin, looking back at the land where they lived. But Elizabeth had carefully made that day disappear from her thoughts, like ironing out a crease in a shirt.

There it was again, though, crisp and clean.

She and Uncle Paul playing soldiers with dead matches. Her mother and Frances, swimming in circles, their heads bobbing up and down in the shiny thick water. The splashes they made with their arms, like the sound of falling tennis balls. Matilda digging in the sand, and running away, Matilda always running away.

And then they were crying, all of them. Everyone in the whole of the Basin was crying. The trees were tall and the trunks were white and the cliffs were huge and they heard a scream and everyone rushed forward and they found him. Their father was hanging from the tallest tree in the Basin, with a rope he had brought in the picnic basket under the sausages and bottles of beer and the tomato sauce. He hanged himself, like a murderer is hanged in prison.

"Why, why, why?" said their mother, on her knees on the ground next to where he lay when they lifted him down just in time, her head on his heart.

It's the war, everyone said, the war, it's nobody's fault, nobody's fault, it's too much, it's too hard, come away, come away now. But why, why, how, sobbed their mother, if only I'd known.

Elizabeth had known.

She had seen him. She knew. She could have done something. She had seen him that morning, packing the rope at the bottom of the picnic basket. He hadn't seen her, he didn't know anyone was watching. He had pushed the rope down in a neat spiral like a snake, under the tartan blanket when he thought no one was looking.

Elizabeth had seen him but she hadn't said anything. She had hardly thought anything. She hadn't understood. But she should have. She should have told her mother, she should have told Uncle Paul. They could have stopped him.

On the ferry going home, they had all sat together in the Ladies' Saloon, except for Matilda. They sat on top of each other like a bundle of parcels and no one said anything. That's when it started, thought Elizabeth, my greensickness. She saw the marks on her father's neck from the rope, and she began to go green.

Her father hanged himself but he didn't die. Nothing could kill him, not even himself. Down in the dark hallway he had crawled on his hands and knees, banging the floor with his fist, that night he came home at last when the war had ended. Elizabeth had seen him then too, banging the floor and weeping like a child, and she had stared in the darkness.

Her father said she had to go back to school, back to the world of words.

Ja nie chat chu. I do not want to go.

"But I won't go back," Elizabeth said calmly. "I don't want to go."

Now at their own beach, with the waves lapping at her feet over the tops of her sandshoes, she saw herself turning green again like the glass of a lemonade bottle, and curved and stiff but somehow molten as well.

I am a glass bottle, she realized without surprise. I have

turned into glass. I can throw myself into the Pacific Ocean and I will float. I will float all the way around the world, even as far as Russia. I will float as far as my father's ship, and he will bend down and pick me up and shake the water off me.

Then he will take the cork from the lid and inside he will find a little piece of paper folded up in a scroll. He will take it out and unroll it, and then he will see written on it in tiny words, so small he will need to use his telescope to read them, he will see that it will say *Ja nie chat chu*.

She stepped right into the water. The only people on the beach were far enough away not to care what she was doing. She walked further into the freezing water, until her feet were nearly numb, until it was as though she didn't have feet.

Soon I won't feel anything at all, thought Elizabeth with relief. She stepped right into the water up to her knees, but she only felt cold, cold and colder. It hurt, deep down into her bones.

Then she heard something resounding from a distance, back towards the house. It was a crack, a banging sound. She looked up.

A cloud moved in the big sky and there was a boat with its white angular sails and the world around her was enormous, quite enormous. And quite suddenly, she didn't want to be cold any more.

Twenty-two

EASTER TUESDAY, 20 APRIL 1954

THE FRONT DOOR SLAMMED. Uncle Paul was back. He'd been at the pub and he was whistling. He was a good whistler, when he was in the mood. He was whistling "Happy Birthday to You".

"It's nobody's birthday," pointed out Matilda.

It was dull without Frances and Elizabeth, and her mother asleep in bed, waiting for their father to come home.

"More's the pity," replied Uncle Paul, unfazed. "But it must be somebody's, somewhere in the world. Your mum still asleep?"

He didn't wait for an answer. She watched him tiptoe to their mother's bedroom and knock lightly on the door. Then he pushed it open, went in and shut it behind him.

Matilda stared at the closed door. She could hear their mother's voice, muffled from inside.

"You don't understand anything, do you?" said Floreal.

"Shut up!" shouted Matilda, leaping to her feet.

"Your father's never coming home," said Floreal.

Matilda swung around in a fury.

"Never!" repeated Floreal. "Never never."

Matilda felt so angry she thought her blood might burst out of her skin. She ran over to the radio in the living room and switched it on. She turned up the volume as loud as it would go. The deep, huge voice of the man inside filled up the room like a rush of water.

"Go away!" she bellowed at Floreal, to make herself heard over the top of the noise. She flung her arm and pointed at the soft round cloth at the front of the radio. "Go back in there and never come out again!!"

The door to their mother's room flew open and Uncle Paul came stamping out.

"What on earth are you doing, Matilda? Turn it off at once!"

"I won't!" yelled Matilda. She stood herself in front of the radio dial. "I won't!"

She glared at him, and he glared back. The voice in the radio seemed to gather strength and become even louder. Uncle Paul raised his hand, she thought he was going to hit her. But before anything could happen, they heard a banging coming from outside the house on the street, CRACK!

"What – for God's sake!"

Uncle Paul went at once to the window and moved the curtain aside.

"Get down!" he ordered, waving at her.

"What is it?" Matilda was frightened.

Uncle Paul bent down and switched the radio off. Matilda, on the floor, crawled over to the low living-room window and rested her nose on the sill to see what was happening.

BANG! BANG!

Their mother came out of the bedroom.

"What is it? What's going on?"

"It's your neighbour," said Uncle Paul, sounding bewildered. "Can you believe it? He's got a gun!"

The neighbour? Matilda peered out. There, on the street in the golden daylight, was the mad old man in his slippers and dressing gown, his gun in one hand and his bright, silver Japanese sword waving about in the other. He was at the front gate of the big yellow house, shooting up into the air.

BANG! went the gun again, and SWISH went the sword.

The mad old man had such a strange look of joy about him, spinning around on the pavement as though he were dancing. Matilda was transfixed.

"He's going to kill someone! Do something, Paul! Do something!"

Matilda looked up at her mother. What did she say?

BANG!

"Do something, Paul!"

Do something. Do something. But Uncle Paul did nothing. He stood at the window, staring, hands in his pockets.

Do something! Matilda had shouted inside her head. Do something!

But she was too far away, high in the tallest tree in the Basin. Nobody could hear her.

Matilda saw everything, silver and grey like mirrors, like moths, everything. Up in the tree she saw her father with the rope around his neck, what was he doing? She didn't understand, but she was afraid. What are you doing? She tried to call out to him, but he would never hear her from that far away, he was all alone in the bush with a rope.

But he wasn't alone. Further back in the bush, behind a sandstone rock as big as a man, Matilda suddenly saw Uncle Paul. Uncle Paul! Uncle Paul would help him! Uncle Paul would stop him. He would do something. Do something!

But Uncle Paul did nothing. He stood, stiff as a stone behind the tree, staring, hands in his pockets. He stood there and he did nothing at all, while his brother hanged himself from the branches of a ghost gum.

Matilda saw him. Matilda saw everything. Uncle Paul stood and watched, and he did nothing at all.

"He won't do anything!" Matilda shrieked and she sprang up from under the window into her mother's arms.

"He never does anything! He just stands there, just like he stood there at the Basin watching Daddy with the rope!"

Her mother turned her head, as though it was on a stiff hinge and looked straight into Uncle Paul's eyes. Then the colour of Uncle Paul's face changed so suddenly, from pink to white, it was as though he had died on the spot.

Outside, there was a screeching of brakes. One of the big black cars pulled up with Mr Driver and Mr Passenger and another man Matilda hadn't seen before. In moments they had dived on top of the mad old man and pulled him down on the street. The old man's head hit the ground and his gun clattered on the ground, and there was blood on his forehead and it shone in the sun.

"Stop it!"

Matilda pulled away from her mother and dashed out the front door. The old man lay on the ground, still holding his sword grim and tight in his gnarled old hand. Mr Passenger and the other man were on top of him, squeezing him, while Mr Driver stood beside them, his own gun drawn.

"Don't hurt him!" Matilda punched Mr Driver, with lots of little hard angry punches. "Don't kill him!"

"Jesus Christ," said Mr Driver, snatching at her fists, slipping the gun back in its holster. He started to drag her away, up the driveway.

"Don't kill him!" Matilda was crying now, and her feet gave way. "You shouldn't kill people, it's bad to kill people, it's not allowed!"

"Shhh, calm down, nobody's killing anybody," said Mr Driver. "He'll be all right, don't worry about him, the silly old goat. He could have killed *you*."

Matilda kept punching, she couldn't stop, but Mr Driver didn't seem to mind.

"He's just scared," she wept, punching and punching. "Anyway, it's my fault. I told him you were spies. I told him about the man on the newsreel. He's scared of spies. And Japs. And Red Indians. He's just scared."

She burst into more tears, sniffing and sobbing. She could hear the mad old man's voice mutter something in the background, so they mustn't have killed him after all. But she didn't want to look, she didn't want to turn and see the blood on his old grey head.

Soon an ambulance came and took the mad old man away on a stretcher. The men in the suits and the black hats arranged it all. There was so much noise, their street had never known so much noise. Mr Driver took Matilda into the yellow house, and gave her a big glass of water.

"Drink it up," he said. "I'll have a word with your mother."

Matilda sipped it, sniffed a lot and then she felt a bit better. She looked around her at the house. It was ordinary, with chairs and tables and bookshelves and carpets. Rich, but ordinary.

"Are you really spies?" she asked, when she felt she could speak again.

Mr Driver didn't answer. He fiddled with his cuff link.

"I think I want to be a spy when I grow up," said Matilda, hiccupping. "Do you think I would be a good spy?"

"I think you will be a fine spy," replied Mr Driver calmly. "Just be careful who you make friends with."

Twenty-three

EASTER TUESDAY, 20 APRIL 1954

WHEN FRANCES CAME HOME, she had no more tears left in her and all she felt was tired, very, very tired. She left her scooter lying on the front path and stumbled in. But as soon as she came inside the house, she felt it was different. Something had happened.

Matilda and Elizabeth were together in the kitchen, next to the sink.

"Where have you been?" said Matilda. "Guess what?"

"I don't know," replied Frances. "What?"

"Daddy came home!" said Matilda, almost shouting.

"Really?" said Frances. She felt lit up inside, like a

candle. She glanced at Elizabeth. Was it true?

"It's true," nodded Elizabeth. "He came home. He just walked in the door. We couldn't believe it."

Elizabeth seemed somehow different to Frances, too, like the house. What was it? Her voice, her eyes. Perhaps she wasn't having her nervous breakdown any more, thought Frances with relief, perhaps she was better.

As though she could see what Frances was thinking, Elizabeth smiled at her. She did feel better, she did. It was funny how simple it was, in the end. She had stepped out of the icy water, back onto the land, her legs wrapped in seaweed. She had pressed her feet into the sand and felt relieved of something heavy and hard.

"Come and see!" said Matilda, hopping up and down. "Come and see him! They're asleep."

The three girls stole down the hallway to their parents' bedroom. Elizabeth pushed the door open and they stepped into the half-light. Their father lay on the bed with his big back in the air, and their mother was curled up next to him.

"They look dead," said Matilda in a tiny voice.

They were so still, the two of them, they did look dead. Matilda was frightened. What if they were dead? What if they had lain down on the bed and died?

"But they're not dead, Mattie," said Elizabeth, leaning over the bed. "You can hear them. Listen."

Matilda stepped forward. Elizabeth was right. They weren't dead. Up close she could hear them breathing, as gently as newborn kittens.

182

That's good, she thought, relieved.

On the floor next to the bed was a box. Matilda knelt down next to it. She wanted to show Frances.

"That's what he brought Mummy. It's a present. Look."

She lifted it up. Inside the box, nestled in tissue paper, was a pair of red slippers, embroidered with crimson swirls.

"They're from Japan," whispered Matilda, touching them with her fingertips. "Aren't they beautiful?"

Now she'll be happy, thought Matilda. Now she won't cry any more.

"Did he get anything for us?" asked Frances, more practically.

"Chocolates," said Elizabeth. "Come on."

They left the room, closing the door behind them with a click. The living room was scattered with paper and string from the presents. Elizabeth, Frances and Matilda lounged about and ate chocolates, listening to the evening bird calls and the sound of the tide.

"I wonder what happened to Uncle Paul?" said Elizabeth, after a while.

"He went away," said Matilda.

"But why?" asked Elizabeth. "Why did he go?"

Matilda shrugged. Did Elizabeth know what had happened that afternoon with the old man and the gun? Perhaps their mother hadn't told her. There had been no time. When Matilda returned from the big house next door, her mother had held her hand and stroked it. "Thank you for the lollipop, Mattie," she'd said, so she must have found it, after all, and then their father came home at last, striding through the open door like a giant, his arms full of gifts.

Frances opened her mouth to speak. She had seen Uncle Paul that afternoon, as she roamed about endlessly on her scooter, till she was too tired to keep going. He had run past on the other side of the street, without his hat, as though he was blind and couldn't even see where he was going.

It was strange to see a grown-up running. He had such an odd look on his face, too. He looked – he looked ashamed, thought Frances. He looked so ashamed. She had never seen Uncle Paul look like that. He ran past her, away, away up the hill. She decided to keep it to herself.

"Do you want to listen to the radio?" asked Elizabeth.

"No," said Matilda, very quickly.

Floreal had been so silent since she'd screamed at him to go back in the radio that she hoped, although she could not quite believe it, that he really had gone away. Maybe he's gone to a radio in another person's house, she decided. He can be friends with someone else now, with someone who actually likes him.

"I'm going to be a spy when I grow up," she said, clambering up on the sofa next to Frances.

"You'd be a terrible spy." Frances rolled her eyes. "You can't keep a secret."

"You don't know all the things I know," said Matilda mysteriously.

"Matilda, even you don't know all the things you know," said Elizabeth with a sigh.

There were no more chocolates. Elizabeth, Frances and Matilda sat on the sofa, resting their arms and legs on top of each other. It was a long time since they had lain so close. It reminded Matilda of how they used to get into Elizabeth's bed, and she would hide under the blankets and pretend she was a monster and make them scream.

Matilda stretched herself out, feeling her bones getting longer and longer. In a little while she would be taller than Frances, maybe one day even taller than Elizabeth. Maybe one day she would be the tallest woman in the world and she could join a circus.

"What if Mummy and Daddy were really dead?" she asked. "What would we do?"

"They're not dead, Mattie," said Elizabeth.

"But if they were," persisted Matilda. "Where would we live?"

"We'd live here, of course," said Elizabeth. "Where else would we live?"

We could just stay here? wondered Frances. In this house? How could there be a house of children without a mother or a father? Then she thought of Mark and his mother. How could there be a mother without a child?

"But who would look after us?" frowned Matilda. "We need someone to look after us."

"I would look after you," said Elizabeth.

I *love* Elizabeth, thought Matilda with a rush. I *love* her.

"Would you?" said Frances. She turned and looked at Elizabeth seriously. Would she?

"Well, I'd have to, wouldn't I?" said Elizabeth.

But I do love her, thought Matilda, and it made her feel so strange she jumped off the sofa and ran out through the laundry into the back yard.

The sun had set and it was night-time. Matilda skipped down alongside the grey splintering fence, near the wet patch where she had found her snails. She sank herself into the ground covered by long, thick, prickly fronds of ivy and peered through the cracks.

The yellow house next door was utterly dark. It was as though it had been shut up, and everybody had gone. There were no cars in the driveway. Had they all left, all those people? Could so many people leave just like that, without anyone noticing, without even saying goodbye?

Suddenly Matilda was aware of eyes looking at her through the green, two tiny, shining, slow, black eyes. She pulled herself up against the fence, her heart beating fast. There was a crackling in the leaves.

It's the goanna, she thought at once. The one that had crawled right up to their house that day, slowly moving its legs forward, one after the other, the one that Uncle Paul frightened away. Half of her was afraid, like her father, but the other half of her was excited. Perhaps this time she would catch it!

"Pssst," she hissed, moving slightly forward. But the eyes disappeared into the wet leafy darkness.

The earth smelt strong to Matilda and full of things growing and dying all at the same time. She stood up against the fence between the two houses. She had so many thoughts in her head.

She thought about the grey-green tangled bush at the end of her street, full of cowboys and Red Indians, waiting with their guns and their bows and arrows. She thought about the Japs and the Germans and the shining sword and chocolate biscuits, and the Argonauts sailing across the ocean, and the silver trail of snails on cardboard. She thought about the swirling lollipop with every colour in the world, and the old man's head on the pavement with blood trickling out from it, and the princess in the film, "How do you do, so glad you could come, how do you do" and the wonderful butterfly bathroom and poor little Karen and her beautiful red shoes. She thought about the sad smiling man with his chess set and the newsreel and her tennis ball, up and up and up in the air, high as the tallest tree in the Basin, and Uncle Paul with his hands in his pockets, his lock of grey hair that flopped over his face, and her mother's red shoe falling down down down into the deep green bush for ever.

Then she remembered the shoebox that their father had brought home with her mother's present inside.

"That would be good for another snail hotel," said Matilda to herself. "Just the right size."

Matilda! she heard someone calling, Matilda! Where are you, where are you, Matilda?

When I grow up I'm going to go around the world! thought Matilda.

She would, she would. Not on a boat, on a plane. She would fly around the world. She held her arms straight out on either side, like an aeroplane.

"Around the world!" she shouted, running up and down the dark back yard.

Matilda! Where are you, Matilda!

All the radios inside all the houses in all the world were humming together, and the sky was filled with electricity. And Matilda was not afraid at all.

The Sydney Morning Herald

Man Shot Dead In Arcade

An unidentified middled-aged man was shot dead in the shooting gallery of a penny arcade in George Street, Haymarket, last night.

Police were told the man entered the arcade about 7.10 p.m., went to the shooting gallery, and paid for three shots.

He was handed a rifle and a few seconds later attendants heard a report.

The man fell to the floor with the rifle falling to the ground beside his body.

The bullet had entered his head.

A Roman Catholic priest, Father J. Dinneen, who was staying at an adjacent hotel, was called and administered the last rites.

The man died soon after the ambulance arrived.

Police are satisfied that he was not the victim of foul play and there were no suspicious circumstances.

MRS PETROV CHOOSES AUSTRALIA

DRAMATIC SCENE AT DARWIN

Diplomat's Wife Will Rejoin Husband

Mrs. Evdokia Petrov decided in Darwin yesterday morning not to return to Russia, but to stay in Australia.

She has been granted political asylum and will rejoin her husband, Mr. Vladimir Petrov, who is "somewhere in Australia" awaiting the Royal Commission into Soviet espionage in Australia.

The Sydney Morning Herald

Mrs. Petrov Relaxes In Garden

DARWIN, Tuesday.— Mrs. Petrov spent to-day relaxing at Government House, in the care of Mr. and Mrs. Reg Leydin.

Late this afternoon she strolled in the garden and spoke to a policeman.

She even asked whether she could have her hair waved.

Mrs. Petrov, who arrived early this morning in a woollen suit, changed into a summer frock after she had taken refuge at Government House.

She rested on a verandah overlooking the harbour and the Administrator's beautiful garden.

Petrov's Dog Keeps Vigil For Master

CANBERRA, Thursday.— Vladimir Petrov's half-grown Alsatian dog this afternoon took up a lone vigil at the front door of his master's old home in Lockyer Street, Griffith, Canberra.

He lay diagonally across the porch, blocking the way, and growling when anyone came close to him.

Whenever a car passed the gates, he lifted his head.

For most of the afternoon the dog refused to leave the entrance porch even when pieces of meat were dropped in front of him.

However, a reporter was eventually able to entice the dog away from the Petrovs' home.

This morning, the dog chased a line of Commonwealth cars taking members of the Russian Embassy staff to Fairbairn airport.

As one of the cars paused close to the Embassy, the dog stood up at one of its windows, wagging his tail.

When the line of cars moved on, the dog ran back to the empty Embassy.

Later in the morning, he was seen running in different suburbs of Canberra.

> *Tuesday*, APRIL 20, 1954 <

Cinesound Special ! !

Mrs. PETROV
Sensational Scenes
at Mascot!

Showing from Tomorrow
Morning at STATE, LYCEUM,
VICTORY, CAPITOL and
LYRIC THEATRES
and STATE and WYNYARD
NEWSREEL THEATRETTES

Acknowledgements

While the people and events in this novel are imaginary, the newspaper excerpts are taken directly from the *Sydney Morning Herald*, the *Sun* and the *Sun–Herald* of the dates stated. I gratefully acknowledge the *Sydney Morning Herald* and Australian Associated Press for granting permission to reproduce these extracts.

The extracts from "The Red Shoes" by Hans Christian Andersen are from *The Complete Hans Christian Andersen Fairy Tales*, edited by Lily Owens, Gramercy Books, New York, 1996, pages 450–3.